PURPLE MIST

- an out-of-this-world adventure!

by Heather Flood

**SECOND EDITION OF PURPLE MIST, containing
five extra chapters.**
Published in January, 2020. Copyright Heather Flood

The right of Heather Flood to be identified as the author of
this work is confirmed in accordance with the
Copyright, Patents and Designs Act.
**COVER IMAGE is based on a picture by WYATT
RYAN on UNSLPASH which has been slightly modified.**

**FORMATTING of the covers and contents by
DINY VAN KLEEFF,** the author of 'A Nurturing Way to Teach
Your Child to Read' and 'FREEN: The First Truth'.

ISBN: 9798604879894

DEDICATION

Many thanks to my dear husband Tony Flood, the author of fantasy adventure 'SECRET POTION', who takes time off from writing his own books to edit mine.

Our books are featured on www.fantasyadventurebooks.com and www.celebritiesconfessions.com

CHAPTER 1

My name is Annique Sheldon. I considered myself to be an ordinary schoolgirl until incredible things began to happen and my worst nightmares started to come true.

My whole world was changed beyond belief on my thirteenth birthday. But let me turn back the clock to five years earlier - the day I discovered I had special powers.

I was hurrying home from school along a country lane in Chobham, Surrey, trying to avoid my three tormentors, Fizz, Stacie and Nicola.

Nicola and I had been friends for a while, but when Fizz joined our class everything changed. Fizz was a bully and soon got Nicola and Stacie to join her in picking on other pupils – usually me!

I no longer had any friends because these three horrid girls would be nasty to anyone they saw speaking to me. Their favourite trick was to call me names.

Determined to ignore them, I continued on my way home, but Fizz grabbed my bag and ripped it off my shoulder, while Stacie and Nicola cheered her on. She swung it violently and the bag, containing all my school books, thudded against my head.

I staggered backwards, rubbing the painful spot above

my left ear.

"You're ugly, *Antique* Sheldon. You've got strange purple eyes and you smell of fish," taunted this tall, thin, squinty-eyed girl, who liked nothing better than to make my life hell.

It amused Fizz to ridicule me and call me '*Antique*' instead of '*Annique*'. I hated her and the snotty-nosed Stacie and pimply Nicola. The spots on Nicola's chin always looked like they would burst at any minute - it was a disgusting sight.

Fizz - that was her nick-name because she preferred it to Felicity - did not care about my pain. Instead of stopping this uncalled for attack, she poked me hard in the chest with one of her bony fingers. The other two joined in, pushing and shoving, until I fell, hitting my head on the ground. The throbbing was so bad that I thought I was going to be sick.

When I looked up Fizz was holding my bag. "There's only junk in here - I'll be doing you a favour if I empty it on the ground," she gloated, starting to unzip it.

"Don't do that," I yelled, trying to stop her but my head ached so much that my eyes began to water.

"Aw, look, poor little Antique is crying," scoffed Fizz.

As my eyes cleared, the feelings of pain and humiliation gave way to an all-consuming anger. I glared at her and a strange *purple mist* appeared in front of me.

Fizz, suddenly surrounded by the mist, was lifted off the ground. She dropped the bag as she began to float into

2

the air, screaming.

"What yer doing up there?" Nicola screeched, seeing her friend rise higher and higher until she hovered above our heads.

"Nufink, stupid - get me down!" Spinning around in the mist, her arms flapping in panic, Fizz shouted: "Help me!"

Stacie leapt in a vain effort to grab hold of one of her friend's legs.

Climbing to my feet, I rushed over to help as the airborne girl continued to wave her arms like a large bird.

Another searing pain behind my eyes caused me to blink. In that instant, she dropped several feet. I recovered sufficiently to tug at Fizz's coat, helping Stacie to pull her down. She landed with a thud in the mud on the wet grass verge.

"Leave me alone, you freak," Fizz shouted at me, climbing to her feet. "Did you do that?"

"No...I don't think so," I mumbled. But my hesitant answer obviously didn't convince Fizz.

"I'll get you for this, Antique. I'll make you suffer."

I picked up my bag and ran as fast as I could the rest of the way home, crashing through the red front gate to my small terraced house. Fumbling in my bag for the door key, I pushed it into the lock, tripped over the step, slammed the door behind me, and rushed up the stairs to my room. I threw myself onto the bed and pulled the duvet up over my head.

Stella, my mother, called to me from downstairs, but I was too afraid to get off the bed as my legs felt like jelly.

My heart thumped in my chest as I went over what had just happened. Was it really me who'd created the purple mist and made Fizz float up into the air? Maybe they were right: I *was* a freak.

CHAPTER 2

"Are you okay, Annique? What's the matter?" Stella said as she came into my room, bending over me to feel my forehead. I'd always suffered from horrible migraine headaches, so I thought she would just give me a pill and then leave me to sleep.

But this time she stared suspiciously into my watery eyes and asked: "Have you been crying? Are those bullies at school troubling you again? I will have another word with your teacher, Miss Gibbons."

"No, please don't, Stella - it wasn't the bullies," I lied, not wanting to tell her what had happened.

I lied a lot in those days. If Stella came up to the school the bullying would get worse, as it did the last time. She never saw the bruises on my arms where they'd punched me.

"I just have a headache, Stella." I really felt guilty telling her lies, but how could I say that I'd lifted someone into the air with a *purple mist* that seemed to come from my eyes? She'd never believe it.

Stella went to get me the usual pill, a glass of water and a damp flannel, which she gently placed on my forehead.

"You must let me know if you have more problems at school," Stella whispered reassuringly. "I know you worry about your school work, but there's no need. You got very high marks in your last report." Stella stroked my cheek softly and then slipped quietly out of my room.

I lay on the bed, my head throbbing as I thought about Fizz's threat and how she would get her revenge on me.

CHAPTER 3

Sitting on my bed later that evening after dinner, I tried as hard as I could to recreate the **purple mist**, making up little verses that I thought might help.

'**Purple mist** *in my eyes - lift me up into the skies.*'

'**Purple mist** *return to me - let me fly like a bumblebee.*'

All right, I know what you're thinking, but my eight-year-old imagination was fired up, especially as two days earlier I'd been to see the second Harry Potter film, the Chamber of Secrets, with my parents, Stella and Graham.

I loved all the wizards and strange characters, especially as my parents were a bit odd, too, and insisted on me calling them by their first names.

We'd queued with lots of kids dressed as witches and wizards. Stella and I had black pointy hats and cloaks on. We'd persuaded my bald-headed father Graham to wear a white wig so that he looked like Lucius Malfoy. Graham had refused to join us in buying toy wands which Stella and I waved at each other while uttering silly spells. I *really, really* wanted some powers like Harry, my *superhero*.

The bullies wouldn't pick on me if I had *powers* like him, would they?

Going over to my bookshelf, I found the Harry Potter novel Stella had bought me. If only I could go to Hogwarts! Surely, my purple eyes and long black hair would be regarded as normal there.

Turning the pages of the book, I came across some of the spells Harry and the other wizards had used. Pointing my wand up at my bedroom light, I tried to cast one of my own by chanting 'LUMAS'. Nothing happened so I decided to stare into the mirror on my bedroom wall, this time chanting 'COLOVARIA', the colour changing spell, hoping that the purple mist would appear.

I stood looking at my image staring back at me, and repeated 'COLOVARIA' but there was no response - no purple mist. I tried several times, finally making up one of my own chants.

"PURPLE MISTECUS!" I exclaimed, swishing my wand furiously around the room.

Nothing!

All the excitement I'd felt earlier disappeared. I slumped back onto my bed in a heap of frustration and angrily threw my wand across the room. I now doubted I possessed special powers, but had no idea who or what else could have made Fizz fly up into the air.

*****

That night I was haunted by a nightmare - but it wasn't about my tormentors.

Instead, I saw a vision of a beautiful woman, wearing

a crown and holding out her hand to me. But as I approached her she staggered backwards, frantically clutching her throat, and the crown fell from her head.

I woke up with a start, got out of bed shaking and stood by the window. Outside a cloud was drifting over the moon's ghostly pale face. It sent a chill down my back as I wondered if there was another moon somewhere - a purple moon.

CHAPTER 4

The next day after school Fizz and her gang were waiting for me outside the school gates.

"Here comes the *witch*, the *weirdo*," they taunted.

Fizz came towards me, glaring menacingly into my eyes. "It's payback time. But first I want to know how you played that trick on me yesterday."

My heart began to race and, in desperation, I began bluffing. "I can do magic - and if you touch me again I'll make snakes grow on your head." I put my hands out in front of me, wiggled my fingers and mumbled something under my breath, as if I were casting a spell.

Squinty Fizz took a step backwards, but the larger pimply-nosed Nicola came forward with her fists tightly bunched, ready to punch me. Stacie followed her and Fizz, seeing that her friends were willing to back her up, launched an attack on me. She grabbed my long hair and yanked it hard, sending pain rippling through my head and bringing tears to my eyes.

"Get off me, you ugly bitches," I shouted as the deep *purple mist* suddenly returned and everything in front of me changed colour.

This time all three of them flew up into the air. They

screamed with fear, and pleaded with me to let them down. I could only look on in disbelief as they spun around in mid air.

I blinked hard to try to clear away the mist and instantly the terrified trio came crashing down on the grass.

Scrambling to their feet, my tormentors bumped into each other in their haste to get away from me. Nicola tripped, scraping her knee. Seeing blood oozing from it, she shouted: "We're gonna tell on you this time."

"Then I'll turn you all into toads," I shouted back.

They fled, with Nicola lagging behind the other two because of her injured knee.

It had happened again. It seemed the mist appeared when I was in trouble or angry. I laughed while skipping home, feeling elated, superhuman, strong and powerful. I loved *my magic mist.* I'd turned into Supergirl, or, in my case, Purplegirl!

CHAPTER 5

I sat on my bed later that evening attempting to bring back the feelings I'd experienced after the bullies picked on me, but nothing happened, nothing moved. Staring at 'Little Stella', my doll, and 'Baggins', my old teddy bear, I chanted: *"Rise, rise and fly."* Their glass eyes just stared back at me and they remained motionless.

My gaze switched to the school photograph which hung on the wall next to a mirror.

"Fizz, Fizz - what a stupid name," I mumbled crossly. Instantly my eyes began to sting. The mirror showed the whites of my eyes appeared normal but the irises in the centre looked huge. I continued looking at myself, chanting *"Fizz, FIZZ"* louder and louder. Within seconds thousands of sparkling particles of purple dust appeared in front of me.

I'd done it! I'd reproduced the purple mist. All I had to do in future was say my enemy's name in anger. Surely these **powers** would put an end to Fizz and her gang bullying me.

*****

I was tempted to tell Stella and Graham, but decided against it. Graham had always worked from home and very rarely came out of his den to speak to Stella or me before my bedtime. When he did he was usually a bit grumpy so Stella would give him one of his special biscuits that she kept in a tin just for him. The biscuits were the only thing that seemed to cheer him up. I tried one once and had to spit it out because it tasted like caster oil. Yuk!

As my confidence grew, I used my levitation powers to play little tricks on my three tormentors.

I made Stacie's glasses move up and down her nose and Nicola's pencil case rise off her desk, then fall on the floor. Whenever Fizz started to approach me during play time, I made her short brown hair stand up as though she'd had an electric shock. She turned and ran!

I wanted to laugh and shout out *"GOT YOU!"* but I didn't want to give myself away to everyone. So I kept quiet even after repeating the pencil case trick which resulted in Miss Gibbons telling Nicola not to be so clumsy.

Fizz and her gang did not bother me again - they were the ones who were scared now, not me!

CHAPTER 6

I remember practising my powers at home, making books, pens, socks and other items fly around my bedroom. But disaster struck one day when my mother caught me.

She'd come into my room with some freshly ironed clothes. My shoes were whizzing around and one of them hit her! She dropped the laundry and jumped back in surprise, rubbing her head.

"What's going on?" she shouted, ducking to avoid the other shoe.

When Stella was cross she had the stare of a Gargoyle, her green eyes flashing with a red rim, I kid you not. I've never seen anything like it. This always stopped me in my tracks because it was a signal that there would be trouble ahead. And her eyes were now flashing wildly! Perhaps she had powers, like me.

"I'm sorry, Stella. But I can make things float around - look it's easy. I have *powers*."

I sent a pen flying off the bedside table and made a glass of water hover over her head. I was so pleased with myself, but another look at Stella's face suggested that telling her might have been a big mistake.

"Stay there and pick up that washing," she ordered,

turning and running down the stairs.

I put the washing neatly on the bed and sat next to it, wondering how my parents would react if they knew I could do *more* than just levitate small things around my bedroom. I could also *lift* people off the ground!

"Come downstairs, Annique," Stella called. "We want to talk to you."

When I went into the lounge, my father removed his glasses and looked at me sternly. His thick grey eyebrows were drawn together in a scowl as he brushed his left hand over his bald head and sighed.

"Stella tells me you can make things float around your room, Annique."

"Yes, I have **powers**, Graham," I said, feeling very grown up, convinced he would be impressed.

He looked at Stella for a few seconds, then turned back to me.

"You must keep these powers, as you call them, secret, Annique. Can we trust you to do that?"

Whatever Graham said was law in our house. He never budged when he made up his mind or set a punishment. So I stood biting my lip as he continued.

"These *powers* must not be shown to others. We could all be in danger if the wrong people found out."

This was not what I had expected him to say.

"Do you mean Fizz and her gang? They already know, and think I'm a *witch,* but don't worry - they're too scared to tell on me."

I laughed until I saw Graham's face turning grey.

"Annique, you don't realise how serious this is," he lectured. "If certain people found out you had this ability they might take you away from us. But you're not a witch - your grandmother could do this levitation, too, by producing a purple mist. It was not uncommon where she came from. She could also hypnotise people just by making eye contact with them, but she was not a witch."

"Where did she come from, Graham?"

"Let's just say that your grandmother's family lived in a far-away place where they talk, dress and behave completely differently."

"Do you mean Scotland? We've just been learning all about Mary Queen of Scots at school, and Scotland's a long way from England, isn't it? They must be a lot different from us, with bagpipes, kilts and the Loch Ness Monster."

"Not Scotland," Stella replied patiently. "It's much further away than that. Your grandmother was from a far off place many thousands of miles away."

"Where?"

"That's enough questions, Annique. This must remain *our secret*. We must be careful that we don't tell other people. Do you understand?"

"Yes, Stella," I said, not understanding at all. "Can I hypnotise people, too?"

"Get that thought right out of year head, young lady!" Graham instructed.

Stella smiled at me. "Graham and I will explain everything when the time is right. Meanwhile, we will start to show you how to use the purple mist properly so that you don't go misusing it. We'll begin tomorrow."

Stella took my hand and Graham went back to reading his newspaper.

"But what good are these powers, if I can't use them on the school bullies?"

Graham looked up from his paper. "As Stella has told you, everything will be explained to you in due course. Try to be patient. And don't go practising your powers without our permission."

"But Graham, don't you realise how great this is? It's not the usual thing people do, is it? I can perform magic."

"It's not *magic*, Annique," said Stella, bending over me, her eyes beginning to glisten with a familiar rosy red hue. "It's a gift that must not be misused." That was a warning to me to persist no further.

Looking at my parents' stern faces, I promised not to use my *powers* until they gave me their permission. But my fingers were crossed behind my back! Well, I wasn't going to let Fizz and her gang bully me again, was I?

CHAPTER 7

Stella and Graham were true to their word, and taught me how to have more control over my *'magic mist'*.

"Why is it purple, Graham?"

"Your eyes are purple, Annique."

"So if my eyes were green, would I see a green light?"

"Yes. But no one else can see it so vividly - just you when you direct it at something."

I turned to my mother. "Your eyes sometimes have a red ring round them, Stella, so does that mean you can do the same as me?"

"No," she replied abruptly, turning to look at Graham.

"Come with me," he said, and we went into the garden behind the shed.

"Imagine holding the mist in your hands, Annique. Concentrate very hard, and by the way, we don't call it *mist* - it is called Falarge. It will grow stronger if you are fully focused."

I thought of my old enemy's name, *Fizz*, and instantly the purple light appeared in my eyes.

An image of her sneering face came into my mind and the purple became so dark it was almost black.

"Hold out your hands, Annique."

When I looked into my palms they began to tingle and glow. As I stared more intensely a spinning ball of light formed between them.

"What should I do now?" I asked, panicking as the ball of light spun and pulsated between my hands. "It's burning - I can't hold it."

"Focus, Annique. Your fear is making you imagine it's hot. Think of it as a tennis ball, and throw it at that flowerpot." Graham pointed across the garden.

Taking several deep breaths to calm myself, I became aware that the ball was no longer hot, though a tingling sensation between my palms increased like little needles. I aimed at the flowerpot, but the ball would not leave my hands.

"Just concentrate on the pot, don't be frightened," urged Stella, who'd come to join us.

I had to make a big conscious effort to do as she said, trying so hard that my head ached. Suddenly the ball of light shot from my hands, exploding into the ground and leaving a very big hole where the flowerpot had been.

I jumped around with delight - until I saw the old couple who lived next door looking out of their bedroom window. Stella obviously noticed them, too. "That's enough for today," she said sternly to Graham. "She can practice again when the neighbours are out."

Graham sighed. He didn't argue with Stella, however, and returned to the house, calling over his shoulder: "I'm going to the newsagents to get a copy of this month's

Science News."

"You did hear what I said, didn't you Graham?"

"Yes, Stella."

"We don't want the neighbours to see!"

"No, dear. We'll avoid the neighbours like the plague."

CHAPTER 8

Not long after witnessing the mini explosion in our back garden the next door neighbours moved. They'd never been very friendly and hardly spoke to us, so we didn't miss them.

Their house stood empty for a while, but in mid-summer a furniture van arrived, and new people moved in - Lee and Kirsty Wellington and their son Antony from Swindon. He was quite small and skinny, with a few freckles above his nose. His shoulder-length fair hair was longer than mine and when I first saw him walking down the path next door I thought he was a girl.

I got back from school one afternoon to find the new neighbours were sitting in our kitchen having tea. Stella introduced me.

"Hello, it's very nice to meet you," said Kirsty, a warm smile spreading over her pretty face.

I smiled and mumbled "Hello" to Kirsty, her husband and son. Then, short of breath after running some of the way home in the rain, I tucked my wet hair behind my ears and went upstairs to quickly change out of my uniform.

Returning to the kitchen, I sat at the table and helped myself to a custard cream, then watched Antony dunk a peanut cookie up and down in his orange juice until half of it fell to the bottom of the glass. A peanut floated to the rim and he fished it out with his fingers. '

'Ugh, I don't think I'm going to like him. How could he dunk a biscuit in orange juice! But perhaps that's what people did in Swindon!' Antony didn't speak much, either, and just seemed to stare, making me feel awkward.

His dad Lee was friendly enough, and asked me what my school was like. "OK," I said without enthusiasm. My inadequate answer made us both smile, and I noticed his fair hair flopped over his eyes, like Antony's.

During the next few days Stella and Kirsty spoke regularly over the garden fence, sometimes in almost a whisper, which seemed very odd.

"Don't be so silly - of course we are not whispering," Stella replied when I asked her what they were being so secretive about. I didn't believe her.

Once I opened the kitchen window quietly and tried to hear what they were saying. But Stella soon became aware that I was there. "Shut the window, Annique. It's rude to eves-drop," she said.

However, I had managed to hear something very interesting before having to close the window: *"We'll tell her everything when she's older."*

What were they hiding from me? I eventually plucked up the courage to ask Stella about my special powers and why I couldn't mention them.

"It's not something you should draw attention to, is it,

Annique? You don't want people to be scared of you or think you're weird, do you?"

"But what about my grandmother?" I persisted. "Graham said it was normal for people where she came from to have these powers. Where did she come from?"

Stella trotted out her usual answer. "When the time is right I'll tell you, Annique. Now don't keep bothering me."

She put on her pink apron and busied herself washing up the dirty dishes in the sink. As she did so, she sang loudly, along with music blasting out from her radio. This caused Graham to stamp on the floor above. It obviously wasn't the 'right time' for me to quiz Stella any further.

CHAPTER 9

Stella invited Kirsty over to our house quite often, and sometimes Lee and Antony came with her.

Antony had started school and was put in the same class as me because his birthday was just two months before mine. He still didn't talk very much, but I thought I'd make an effort to be friendly, seeing as Stella and Graham were getting on so well with the Wellingtons.

"Do you fancy playing hide and seek?" I asked him.

"Not really," he replied, taking out a piece of chewing gum and popping it in his mouth. He held out the packet. "Want some?"

"No thanks. Stella would throw a fit if she saw me chewing gum."

"Why do you call her Stella?"

"That's just the way she likes it. I've always called my parents Stella and Graham."

"Sounds a bit strange to me. They're your Mum and Dad so why can't you call them that?"

He was beginning to wind me up, especially as he was right - I'd always wanted to call them Mum and Dad.

"What about skipping?" I asked, trying to change the subject.

"No way, that's for girls. How about us playing with your exploding light ball?"

"*WHAT!!*"

"You know, that exploding light ball you were using the other day. That's awesome."

He must have seen me practising with my mist. I had to think quickly or Stella and Graham would be furious with me for letting someone else see my powers.

"Oh, *that* ball - it burst."

"That's a shame," he muttered and walked away, turning to look through our shed window.

"What's in here?"

"Nothing much, just lots of spiders."

"We could make a den in here," he said, pulling the door open.

"Okay, that's a good idea, I'll go and ask Stella."

That afternoon we began turning the old shed into our den. Stella swept all the spiders and cobwebs out, and we were handed two buckets of soapy water to clean it. Kirsty gave us some old scatter cushions to sit on and we hung posters on the walls. It really looked great when we'd finished.

We put signs on the door which read:

'KEEP OUT - SECRET DEN - ENTER AT YOUR PERIL'

It was great to come home after school and sit together, writing our homework. During the summer holidays we played snap or dominoes and sometimes just read comics. When Antony went away on holiday with his parents for a couple of weeks I really missed him.

We became good friends, walking to school every morning once the new term started in September. We shared several interests and found that we both wanted to go horse riding at the local stables. But Stella said 'no'.

I told Antony all about the bullies. Whenever we passed them he moved protectively in front of me, and they didn't trouble us. It was quite funny really, because I knew it was me they were afraid of, not skinny Antony. They would have made mince meat of him. But it was nice to have a friend who'd stick up for me.

We spent most of the remaining warm evenings sitting in the den surrounded by posters of Harry Potter, Chelsea football players and fast cars.

Antony taught me to play another card game called 'fingers', where you have to predict how many tricks you can win by sticking out your fingers. I laughed as he called out: "Okay, boys and girls, how many tricks can you win - show your fingers NOW!"

We played for sweets, mostly jelly babies and sherbet lemons. Antony still had the annoying habit of chewing gum, and I told him off when I began to notice bits of it stuck on the walls of our den.

"That's disgusting, Antony. If Stella found it she'd kill you."

"Okay, sorry, Kidda." he said. Antony liked calling me 'Kidda' because he was two months older and had grown slightly taller than me, but I got my own back by nicknaming him 'Old Boot' after his Wellington surname.

He seldom took much notice of my rebukes and I still occasionally discovered odd pieces of gum stuck behind the door frame.

CHAPTER 10

Antony and I both transferred to Canningham High School when we were eleven.

Despite his increase in height, he was still quite thin, with freckles over his nose, like his mum. He'd had his hair cut shorter, whereas I'd let mine grow until it swung around my shoulders. It looked like a silky dark cloud. Well, that's what I told myself after I'd brushed it 50 times every morning.

Stella refused to let me have lipstick. She said 'no' very firmly, but instead bought me a pale pink nail varnish to wear at weekends.`

I hadn't told Antony about my mist yet, but one day he saw it for himself. As we sat doing our homework in the den, a large black spider crawled out from under one of the cushions and ran towards me. I was scared of spiders and, after scrambling out of the way, quickly surrounded it with my purple mist, levitating it in the air.

"What the hell's that?" Antony yelled, trying to put distance between us, but only succeeding in tripping over my bag and landing face down.

My outburst of laughter didn't prevent me keeping the spider firmly trapped in the mist with my purple gaze.

"I have *powers*, Antony."

"Don't be blooming stupid," he yelled, getting to his feet, clearly shaken.

"I do, *really* – look!" I shifted the mist to position the spider in front of his nose.

"How do you do that?" His mouth fell open in disbelief. I feared he might swallow the spider so I let it drop to the floor where the frightened creature scurried away.

"It's my magic mist. My grandmother could do things like this, too. Do you remember the day you saw me with that spinning ball of light in the garden?"

"You said it was a toy, and had got broken. Hold on, do you mean to tell me that you can conjure up enough power to make things explode?"

"Yes. Stella and Graham told me I must keep it a secret, but I'm so glad you know."

He stood in silence staring at me.

"Don't look at me like that, Antony. It's just something I do - it's just a bit of fun really. I made Fizz float up into the air once."

"What... she knows, too? And your old teachers, do they know? Am I the only one you didn't tell? No wonder those bullies left you alone... and I thought I was protecting you from them. How could you trick me like that?"

He pulled hard on the shed door, forcing it to swing open and crash against the wall as he left. Even though Antony was thin, he had grown into a strong 11-year-old.

"Please don't go, Antony. Only Fizz and her friends know." But he didn't look back and stomped off in a huff.

Luckily Stella was out shopping or I would've had a lot of explaining to do. I'd just shown Antony my powers after promising not to tell anyone else. Yet, despite finally sharing my secret with him, I'd made him angry, and perhaps lost my only true friend.

CHAPTER 11

Antony didn't come round for me the next morning and I walked to school on my own.

I was suddenly confronted by Fizz and her friends, who were on their way to Ash Vale Senior School. "Where's your slave?" she taunted. "Has he found out you're a freak?"

"I thought the freaks were now going to Ash Vale," I retorted.

Fizz stood in front of me, blocking my path, and we glared at each other, neither of us giving way. There couldn't be a better time to discover if I had the power to hypnotise someone by staring into their eyes, even someone with a pronounced squint. I concentrated as hard as I possibly could and willed her to apologise to me.

To my amazement Fizz smiled sweetly and said: "Sorry Annique. I shouldn't have been so rude." She then stood aside to let me go past.

Stacie and Nicola looked gob-smacked.

*****

A few miserable days passed before Stella noticed Antony's absence and asked what had happened to him.

"He's got a cold," I lied. "He'll come round when he's better."

I went out into the den and stood looking through the window at the bird table. Antony used to feed the birds with me every day before school - now I was on my own.

My only companions were a few bees buzzing around the lavender which Stella had planted among the rose bushes. We'd been taught at school how important bees were to us and the food chain on earth. Our kitchen cupboards always had pots of different types of honey. The lavender scent was lovely in our garden in summer, and Stella spent hours outside planting and weeding. She didn't like killing anything with sprays or poisons so sometimes she would collect all the slugs into a jam jar and release them in the local park.

Staring aimlessly at the garden, I heard a noise behind me - and then a voice.

"Okay, I've been thinking..."

I spun round and there was Antony, hands in his pockets, chewing gum, leaning against the door.

"...perhaps you didn't mean to trick me. So tell me everything - when it started, everything."

Antony came closer and took my hand, pulling me onto the cushions. For the next half hour I told him how I'd discovered my powers and used them on the bullies - and what my parents had explained to me. I even told him how I had apparently hypnotised Fizz.

"So Graham and Stella said your grandmother was

from a far off place, but would not tell you where. That could be a country on the other side of the world - or maybe another planet. Wow, that would be cool if it was from another planet."

"Don't be so silly, Antony."

"I'm not being silly. You've inherited these powers from your grandmother so who is to say that she is not from another world? Ask them again, Annique. It's your life, after all. It's like a fairy story in which the young heroine is being denied the truth."

"Oh shut up!" I laughed and threw a cushion at him. "Maybe I'll go to sleep for a hundred years and be woken up by a prince who'll want to marry me."

"Yea, and live happily ever after," he teased. "Parents can be so cagey sometimes. I'm sure mine are up to something, but they won't tell me, either. There's a lot of whispering going on and it stops when I enter the room. But I'll get to the bottom of it, or I'm not your Old Wellington Boot."

We both laughed – happy to be friends again.

CHAPTER 12

"My dad says it's important to learn about the past, He's always going to the library to read old books," Antony said on our way home from school one evening. "Libraries are so cool - they've got books that date back centuries, Why don't you come with me tomorrow?"

"Maybe I will, but surely if you want to know something you can just look it up on Google. Graham lets me use his lap-top when I have homework."

"I like the atmosphere in a library and really enjoy looking at some of the old books. Think how many people have read them before us, Annique. Sitting staring at a screen for hours can be so boring."

We were both doing well at Canningham High, but we needed to keep up the good work because Parent Evening was just a few weeks away. Antony was looking quite fit now he was thirteen. He went for long jogs twice a week and sometimes worked out in our den, pushing aside the cushions and producing up to thirty press-ups.

"How do you do so many?" I asked, impressed.

"My Mum must take the credit."

"Your Mum?"

"Yes, she used to make me do press-ups when I was

naughty. But after a while I enjoyed doing them!"

I preferred to sit in the den in my track bottoms and T-shirts, doing my homework. My favourite subjects were English, art and geography, but I struggled with maths - partly because the teacher, old Mr Potter, was so boring. I'd joined the school choir and met two girls there, Jennifer and Emma, who I really liked. The three of us got on really well, but I spent most of my free time with Antony.

Clever Old Boot was good at everything. I 'hated' him sometimes, especially as several of the girls in our class hung around him at lunch time, especially one called Tiger.

"Does she growl at you often?" I teased.

Tiger obviously had a crush on Antony. I overheard her speaking to a friend as I stood behind them in the queue for lunch. She gushed: "Antony's so dishy and those little gold spots in his grey eyes are like *flecks of gold dust*"

I had to admit Antony looked rather cool, with his distinctive eyes and new short haircut. I secretly hoped he'd noticed I was wearing some lip gloss, as Stella had finally allowed it, but then felt like washing my mouth out with soap for even having such a thought.

"Well Kidda," he said, as we walked home from Canningham. "Have you found out any more about this secret you think your parents are keeping from you?"

"No. Stella won't let on. She just hinted that she might have something important to tell me, but I'd have to wait until my birthday."

"Don't leave it to chance," he advised. "Remind her

35

about it. Make her promise to tell you."

"Okay. I hope it's good news. I wouldn't like to turn into a purple looking Shrek."

"You mean Mrs. Shrek."

We both laughed, but I was becoming a bit apprehensive.

CHAPTER 13

Soon after breakfast on Saturday I went with Antony to the library to obtain books for our school projects. He needed one on ancient Greek artefacts - boring! - and I wanted a couple on science fiction.

I had ordered a book about possible new inventions and I was hoping to find out if anyone had come across coloured particles floating around in the air.

Upon reaching the library, I left Antony in the history section and took the escalator to the second floor.

After collecting my order, I wandered up and down the aisles, browsing at books on science fiction, I was drawn to one with a large moon on its cover.

Suddenly I felt faint as the room seemed to spin. I made a grab for the book shelf to steady myself and closed my eyes, letting the dizziness waft over me and a bitter taste flood into my mouth.

My head throbbed as I was drawn back into what had become a recurring nightmare. My dream always started so well, with me being drawn towards the same lovely lady, in a long white robe and wearing a crown. Once she held me in her arms, her soft cheek pressed next to mine, while we looked up at a purple moon. But this gentle scene turned into one of panic and screams as she was dragged away, ripping those soft memories from my head.

Gasping for breath, I dropped the book on the floor. I recovered my balance, but was left with a raging headache. Would I ever find out why I had these dreams and what they meant?

*****

The next morning as I stood at the back door I heard Stella talking to Kirsty over the fence.

"We don't like her to go far without us," Stella was saying.

"But it's only a few miles away, and it would be a nice treat for Annique," Kirsty persisted.

"I'm taking Antony anyway, so I can make sure they will both be alright."

There was a pause before Stella answered. I was willing her to agree. Finally she said: "OK.

Next weekend, then."

The following weekend Stella and Graham allowed Kirsty to take me horse riding with Antony at a stables not far from the famous Epsom racecourse. It was our first lesson, but Kirsty seemed to be more concerned about me than him.

I didn't want to upset her and hid my indignation until Antony smirked as his mother continued to fuss around me, I could not stop myself glaring at him.

But the horse riding was great fun, and Kirsty

persuaded Stella to let me go with Antony most weekends, as long as I kept up with my homework.

We became very competitive, each desperately wanting to win our races through the woods.

The first time I beat him, he claimed: "I let you win that one, Kidda," It was a double insult because he knew just how much this silly nick-name annoyed me.

"Take care, Old Boot, or I'll *mist* you," I warned him.

I became more and more confident riding my lovely horse Bella and felt completely at ease in the saddle. My friend Emma sometimes joined us as she had been riding since she was nine.

Looking back, I now feel that those were some of my happiest childhood days. Loved and safeguarded, I didn't have a clue what was to happen as I approached my thirteenth birthday.

CHAPTER 14

"Annique what is the matter - is there something wrong with the bolognese?" asked Stella as I sat twirling my fork into the spaghetti.

"I'm just not very hungry, Stella, sorry. Have you heard that Antony's dad is going to America? Antony told me yesterday when we were in the den. It's to do with his father's job. I hope he's not thinking of moving over there."

Graham looked up suddenly and glared at Stella, which made me feel uneasy.

"Now if you two have finished eating I will take the plates," said Stella, refusing to answer my question. "Perhaps you can help me wash up, Annique."

"Okay," I replied, trying to sound more enthusiastic than I felt.

Helping Stella put away the dishes after dinner was always a long job because she was so precise. I was sure she had an obsessive-compulsive disorder as everything had to be exactly in the right place, with cutlery all facing the same way in the drawer, handles on cups to the right. Even the tea-towel had to be folded before it was put into the washing machine and a new one taken out every day.

"It's my job and I like to do it properly," she'd say,

rinsing everything twice. "A clean and tidy ship is a happy ship."

To make matters worse, she insisted that I wore a frilly pink apron, like her. This time I thought she might not notice - I was mistaken.

"Apron on!" she demanded.

"But, Stella, I'm a sailor on a clean and tidy ship, aren't I? And sailors don't wear pink aprons."

Stella's eyes changed from green to bright red, and I knew it was pointless arguing any further. I went to the kitchen drawer which was full of pink aprons and put one of them on.

How strange it was that I could create a 'magic mist' with my purple eyes, but was still scared stiff when she gave me her 'red stare'.

Although Stella had not claimed to possess any powers, I suspected that she had some, too.

CHAPTER 15

Antony called round the following day to ask if I could go riding with him. I couldn't wait to find out the latest news about the trip his father would be taking to America. As he sat in our kitchen he stuffed one of Stella's freshly baked ginger cakes into his mouth.

"Antony, I think you should have asked Stella if you could have one of her cakes, before you started scoffing it. She counts them, you know."

Stella came in while I was speaking and promptly over-ruled me. "That's alright, Annique - he's a hungry lad. You can have another one, dear."

Now if I'd done that she would've had a fit, but because it was *Antony*, she offered him another one on a plate. He tried to thank her, but as he'd still got the first cake crammed into his mouth it came out sounding like "Fank woo."

Despite this, Stella smiled fondly at Antony. I was so annoyed that she only seemed to see his good points and was tempted to tell her about the chewing gum stuck all over the shed.

Antony appeared to read my thoughts as he turned to look at me. He raised his eyebrows appealingly, prompting me to mouth the word '*creep.*'

But his ability to charm Stella had its advantages, and she agreed to let me go horse riding with him even though Kirsty was not available to accompanying us.

*****

The stables were a half hour bus journey from where we lived and that gave me the chance to quiz Antony about his father's trip to America.

"So when is your dad actually going?"

"We're still waiting to hear, but it should be quite soon. Actually we're all going. Dad will be working but for Mum and I it will be a short holiday." He then changed the subject and told me excitedly about how he had scored two goals to help the school football team gain a 2-1 victory.

We soon arrived at the stables and lost little time in saddling our horses, Bella and Crispin.

It was only then that I realised Antony had not told me how long he would be in America.

"I suppose you'll be away at least a couple of weeks."

"Longer than that - almost two months actually."

I was stunned. The shock caused me to miss putting my foot into the stirrup as I attempted to mount Bella, and I nearly toppled over.

"Two months? That long? But surely you won't be allowed to miss school for that amount of time."

"Mum says it shouldn't be a problem. I'll have finished my exams before we go. As soon as things are fixed up she'll give the school the dates and I'll have to tell Beryl that I won't be riding Crispin for a while."

Beryl was the owner of the stables, and Crispin and Bella were her horses, along with four others - Mr. Tea Bag, a dear old chap who we all loved, Bourne Chorus, a sprightly bay filly, and Rhubarb and Custard, two chestnut coloured ponies.

"I'll miss you - two months is a long time. I can't believe it."

"I'll miss you, too, Kidda, but I have to go, and I'm really looking forward to seeing America."

"But what if your dad decides to stay longer or move there?"

"Don't worry, I'm sure he wouldn't want to do that. Besides, how could I possibly give up living next door to a scruffy little kid who follows me everywhere?" he said, laughing as he jumped onto Crispin in one magnificent, show-off manoeuvre. He'd become a really good rider – much better than me.

"You're asking for trouble, Old Boot."

"Let's not waste time, Kidda. The sun is shining and it's a great day for cantering through the woods." With that, Antony sped off.

Bella and I gave chase in time to see Antony making for a wooded area and prepare Crispin to jump over some fallen branches. Oh, how I wished cocky Wellington Boot would misjudge it and topple out of the saddle. I needed a laugh, but he remained in full control.

"Come on slow-coach," he shouted after clearing the obstacle.

"So that's the way you want to play it today, is it?" I called after him, urging Bella to follow at a gallop. The wind caused my hair to whip around my face as I gradually caught up with him.

Seeing me coming up by his side, Antony pulled on Crispin's reins, which resulted in the large black horse swerving in front of Bella.

"Okay Mr. Clever Clogs", I yelled. "You asked for it. A girl's gotta do, what a girl's gotta do."

As if he knew what was coming, he called out: "Don't' you dare, Annique. You'll be sorry, I swear it. I'll tell Stella." But his plea and threat fell on deaf ears. I could already see a glorious purple mist surrounding him and his horse.

Crispin began bucking and prancing, as if he was dancing in thick treacle. Rider and horse rose a few feet off the ground, with the mist swirling around them.

"You devil!" Antony shouted, clinging on desperately, his feet coming out of his stirrups.

"Get me down or..."

"Or what - what *will* you do Mr. Speedy?"

"I'll... I'll...just you wait and see," he stormed, his long legs dangling in the air after coming out of the stirrups.

I let them remain suspended for a few seconds before closing my eyes to stop the mist.

Hearing the thud of Crispin's hooves, as they made

contact with the earth, I opened my eyes again and doubled up laughing. The large black horse galloped off with Antony pitching and swaying, trying to keep his balance.

You know when you get one of those amazing moments in life, well it was one of those I will never forget.

"Yes, yes," I shouted, fist raised in the air, triumphantly. How satisfying it was to put one over on Old Boot.

CHAPTER 16

"Hello Annique," Kirsty greeted me at her front door on the morning our neighbours were due to leave for America. I was surprised to see that she'd had her lovely wavy auburn hair cut short.

"We're in such a rush, dear. *Lee,* can you put the suitcases in the car - *now."*

Antony's father came down the stairs jingling his keys. "Hi Annique, it's a mad house here, I'm afraid. If we aren't ready to leave soon I'll be in big trouble with the Boss." He looked over at Kirsty, then turned and winked at me. Lee had the same sense of humour as his son.

Antony came out of the kitchen and was about to speak to me when his mother brushed past, carrying two bags. "Sorry dear, but we really haven't got time to talk," she said.

Ignoring her, Antony flashed a smile and pulled me into the kitchen.

"Mum's in a flap because we're due to leave in 30 minutes."

"Do you know when you'll be coming back?" I asked.

"Not yet."

"I bet you're going to miss my birthday," I moaned.

"Of course I won't. We'll be back before then."

He pushed the door shut with his foot and stood in front of me. I thought he was going to hug me but we just stared at each other. "Do you promise?"

"Yes, I promise." We both stood looking at each other for a few moments in silence. I felt quite embarrassed until he reached into his pocket and took out some gum, offering a piece to me.

"I don't want your old gum," I snapped, snatching it out of his hand and throwing it into the sink.

"Well, that's not very nice," he sighed, retrieving the gum from the sink and putting it back in his pocket.

"You're disgusting, Antony!"

He turned with a stupid grin on his face. "Now don't go missing me too much, will you?"

"I might go out clubbing with Emma and Jennifer," I answered, not wanting him to think I would miss him at all.

"Good luck with that one, Kidda," he teased. "Somehow I don't think Stella will allow it."

Ten minutes later I stood outside the Wellingtons' front gate and watched as Antony got into the back of his Dad's large Station Wagon. Kirsty told me not to worry. "We'll be back soon," she said, giving me the hug I had not received from her son!

As they drove off Antony looked out of the rear window, waved and actually blew me a kiss.

I blew one to him, too, but he'd already turned around. I felt so fed up I kicked the gate post and stubbed my toe.

CHAPTER 17

Time dragged while Antony was away. I missed his freckled face appearing round the door of our den, the silly grin and the gum chewing. I even missed his teasing and calling me Kidda.

I had lots of homework, but it was hard to concentrate. Walking round our garden in the mornings, I'd lean over the fence and look up at the empty windows next door. It felt eerie, seeing the curtains pulled together - like when our previous neighbours left.

Stella confided that she also found it strange not having Kirsty to chat with each morning.

That made it easier for me to cope. I finally focused on my homework and regularly went to the library for study periods.

But there were times when I felt depressed. With Stella busy and Graham locked in his office, I'd sit talking to teddy Baggins and Little Stella.

One day a charity shop bag was posted through our front door, and that seemed to be the start of a massive clear out by Stella. She became fixated on the task and urged me to join in.

"We have far too much junk," she announced. "You

should sort through some of your things, too. Your bedroom's become quite cluttered."

Trudging up to my room, not really feeling in the mood, I eventually gathered together some of my old things, including a couple of pairs of shoes that no longer fitted, and put them in a bag downstairs.

I noticed that all the shelves in the front room had been cleared. Apart from our TV and the furniture, there were few things left on view. How had Stella done all this in the thirty minutes I'd been upstairs? Was she super human?

"Stella, surely we've given enough to charity."

"Yes, perhaps you're right, Annique. It looks very tidy now, but I still need to go through the paperwork and photos in the draws." She moved towards our cabinet.

"Please don't throw any of our pictures away Stella. I like to look at them, especially the ones we took when we visited Buckingham Palace. *And* there's those we took on our trip to Eastbourne with Antony and his parents. Do you remember we sat on the old cannons at the Redoubt Fort, and then went to Beachy Head to watch the sunset? It was so beautiful."

"Don't worry Annique," she said, taking a bag full of pictures from one of the cabinet draws.

"I'll keep the ones you want, but there are so many here - we need to throw some away."

"But why are you throwing so many things out? We're not moving, are we?"

"We can't stay here for ever," Stella replied.

"So we ARE moving?"

"I didn't say that," she insisted. "But you know my motto, don't you?"

"A clean and tidy ship is a happy ship."

"Not that one. The motto I'm referring to is: Always be prepared!"

CHAPTER 18

Six long weeks had gone by since Antony left and he hadn't even sent me a card. I was getting very cross with him.

One morning while sitting down to breakfast with Stella, and moodily pushing my cornflakes around the bowl, I asked: "Can we go clothes shopping today?"

"Not today, dear. Our next door neighbours have arrived back and I want to see Kirsty later.

Besides, I bought you some skinny jeans last week."

"Antony's back! Why didn't you tell me before?"

"They only arrived early this morning. It's no good rushing over there, Annique - they will be sleeping now."

I gulped down my cornflakes and hurried to my room to brush my hair until I was satisfied it looked okay. Then, staring at my face in the mirror, I noticed my strange purple coloured eyes shone with excitement. This was my lucky day as I didn't have any horrible spots on my face. I wondered if I should wear a dress, but chose a pink blouse that would go well with my new blue jeans.

Looking at the result in the mirror a few minutes later, I wished I had persuaded Stella to let me buy a lipstick, but comforted myself with the thought that I didn't want to appear desperate to see him, did I?

I sat on my bed, repeatedly looking at my watch, until I eventually decided to go into the den. As I approached it I noticed the door was open and rushed inside. There was my dear Old Boot!

"Antony, you're back!" I felt flushed with excitement. But he was slumped in the corner, resting his head in his hands.

"What's the matter? You look awful - what's happened?"

He stood up and walked to the window, brushing the fingers of his left hand through his fair hair. Going to stand beside him, I took his other hand in mine, fearing his answer. When Antony turned towards me, the cheeky grin I was used to seeing had gone, to be replaced by a sad frown. I was convinced he was about to tell me that he and his parents were going to move to America.

"I'm just tired, that's all. It's been a long trip."

I knew he was lying. He kept staring at me as if he'd something more to say. I felt a fluttery feeling of panic in my stomach.

"Please tell me if you're moving to America, I can't stand not knowing. Just tell me."

"What on earth are you saying, Annique? Moving to America? - What gave you that idea?

We're not moving to America. Who told you that?"

"I just thought that as your Dad's job took you there, they might want him to return for good."

"No." But Antony refused to say anything more, and

the silence between us began to feel embarrassing.

"How's your Mum and Dad - did you all enjoy the trip?"

"It was fine," he replied, putting a piece of gum into his mouth and chomping down heavily on it.

"So do you want to go riding? We haven't been for ages"

"Not today."

"You're in a bad mood, Antony. What's up?"

"I can't tell you, Annique. I really can't."

I kicked him in the shins. "Tell me or else."

"Or else what? Don't you dare try that stuff on..."

"I'm *all powerful* like the Wizard of Oz," I snapped, and before he could say anything else I held him in my purple stare. Within seconds he was floating above the wooden floor in the shed. As he flapped his arms and legs about, I took pity and quickly let him land gently on his feet.

At last his mood lifted and we both burst out laughing. Picking up one of the cushions off the floor, he aimed it at my head, and for the next few minutes we had a pillow fight. I hit him so hard with one cushion that it burst open, scattering feathers everywhere.

"*Annique!*" Stella's high pitched voice interrupted us from the kitchen. "It's time for lunch."

We quickly picked up as many feathers as we could and Antony blew one off my nose.

"See you later," he said as we left the den and started

to climb over the fence into his own garden.

"But you *still* haven't told me why you were upset."

He turned and I saw that worried look return to his face. "Go and get your lunch," he said.

CHAPTER 19

My thirteenth birthday was now only a week away and I reminded Stella that I was expecting her to give me some important information, but got little response.

"We'll see," she said.

"And can my birthday treat be a visit to the London Eye? My friend Emma says it's amazing."

"We'll see," she repeated, not even looking up from cleaning the grill.

After school the next day Antony and I went for a smoothie at the local coffee bar.

"What is it with my parents?" I asked him. "Why all the secrecy?"

He shrugged and left me sitting at a corner table while he went to queue for the drinks.

As usual the coffee bar was packed. Two girls from our school were staring at Antony as he passed them, carrying our drinks to the table. I looked icily at the girl with long blonde hair and she raised her eyebrows before sticking one finger up at me. Charming!

Old Boot couldn't resist glancing across at her. I had to admit that she was quite pretty. I had competition! Maybe it was time to do something different with *my* hair and ask

Stella if I could buy an eye liner.

After taking a sip of my smoothie, I tried to pump Antony for information. "Have you any idea what my birthday surprise is going to be?"

"Search me," came the unconvincing reply.

Since his return from America Antony had been acting a bit weird - somehow he was different. He looked older but there was something else. He seemed unwilling to share any of his thoughts with me. Suspicious, eh?

"Our mums are always talking. Surely you must have a clue," I persisted.

He didn't answer but instead reached into his jacket pocket and pulled out a small parcel.

Taking my hand, he gave me a little box wrapped up in silver paper.

"I hope you like it, Annique."

"Ooh, thank you."

I opened the box and inside was a beautiful silver bracelet with a large purple stone in the middle and six tiny purple jewels around the clasp. The stones were almost the same colour as my eyes.

"I love it, Antony," I muttered as he put it round my wrist. "It's wonderful."

"Look, I have one as well." He grinned and pulled up his cuff to show me. The only difference was his had pale grey stones - the colour of *his* eyes.

"They're communication bracelets. Just press the little clip on the side of yours."

It was quite stiff and I pushed it a couple of times before the stone sprang open to reveal the inside, which was whirling around in a circle.

Gazing down into its centre, I suddenly saw Antony's smiling face appear. "I can see you - it's like a little TV screen. Can you see me in yours?"

He pushed the little clasp on the side of his bracelet and I peered over his arm. Just my left eye appeared in the centre as I'd got too close. I pulled my head back until all of my face became visible.

"They're brilliant - is this my birthday present?"

"No - that's still to come. Dad got these bracelets while we were away and said I should give this one to you."

"That was so nice of him. I'll go and thank him later. This means we can see each other on these little screens whenever we like. Stella and Graham used to wear similar looking bracelets but I didn't know what they could do."

"We can talk through them as well," Antony informed me.

"Really? How? Show me."

I was delighted with this wonderful gift. I hadn't been allowed a mobile phone, even though I'd begged my parents for one, but this was even better.

Antony put his thumb under his wrist and pushed another tiny button on the clasp.

The clasp on my bracelet began to vibrate and when I pushed it I heard his voice.

"Hello, Annique. What do you think of this?"

"It's so cool."

I kissed him on the cheek and then went bright red when I realised the two girls from our school had seen me.

*****

The first thing I did when I got home was to show Stella the bracelet.

"Look what Antony's Dad got me, Stella. He bought it in America. Antony's got one, too.

She held my arm and glanced at the bracelet. "It's a communicating device," she said matter-of-factly. "Graham and I each have one upstairs."

"Yes, I've seen them. But I didn't know you used them to talk to each other."

"We haven't worn them for a while because they need recharging. We must get them fixed.

We will need them soon."

'Need them soon, eh?' I thought. But Stella went back to preparing our dinner, smoothing down her pink apron without making any further comment. She was a rather strange person sometimes.

I went to my room and sat on my bed gazing at the bracelet. It was so lovely and, as I looked at the stones, it reminded me of something. I went over to my jewellery box and took out my gold heart-shaped locket. In the middle of the heart was a tiny purple stone - the same colour as the ones on my bracelet.

The locket contained a photo of my grandparents. On the right of the picture was my Grandfather, a tall handsome man, with dark hair, and a big smile. My Grandmother's delicate features and long black hair were similar to mine, and our eyes were the same colour. Stella did not look like either of them. She had short brown hair and green eyes, which glowed red whenever she was cross.

Stella had already told me that both my grandparents died in an accident when I was a baby. I kissed their happy smiling faces in the photo, wishing I had known them, and slipped the heart around my neck.

I promised myself that I would find out more about them and where they had come from.

CHAPTER 20

The day before my birthday Antony and I were walking home from school, sharing a chocolate bar. As I finished licking the delicious chocolate off my fingers, I spotted a girl, with curly red hair, standing on the bridge overlooking the local river.

She was holding a little black dog by the scruff of its neck, and trying roughly to push it into a sack. The struggling animal yelped in panic.

The girl succeeded in getting the dog into the sack, which she began tying at the top. She then swung it around, preparing to fling it into the river.

"Hey you, don't do that," Antony shouted as we ran up to her.

I managed to snatch the wriggling bag out of her hands before she could throw it into the rushing water below. I tore the top open and removed a little puppy with a small white patch on his otherwise black chest. His soft brown eyes stared into mine as he shook and peed over my hand with fright.

"What the hell were you doing?" Antony demanded of the girl, who sneered at us and started to walk away.

"Wait!" called Antony, going after her. "Is he yours?"

Ignoring him, she turned and ran down a slope alongside the end of the bridge.

Antony gave chase, but tripped and fell headlong, hitting his head against a large stone.

He cried out in pain as the girl vanished.

"Antony!" I yelled in alarm as I ran towards him, still holding the little dog. Kneeling in front of him, I saw blood streaming down his forehead.

I grabbed some tissues from my pocket and pressed them against a large gash.

"That looks awful, Antony. Can you stand up?"

"Yes, I think so, but I feel sick."

As he stood he threw up over the side of the road.

"You poor thing. You've turned very pale, Antony. Lean on me."

With me holding on to both Antony and the little dog, our progress was slow, but eventually, after about 20 minutes, we reached the Wellingtons' front gate.

"Oh, I forgot. Mum won't be in," Antony told me. "She goes to her ladies' club on a Friday."

"Let's go and see Stella, then." I pulled open our wooden gate and shouted, "Stella, Stella."

We need your help. Antony's had an accident." The door swung open and my worried mother rushed towards us.

We helped him inside and I put the puppy on the floor after closing the door. The frightened animal ran into the living room and hid behind the sofa.

I quickly followed him. "Don't be afraid. I'm your friend. I won't hurt you."

Stella told Antony to sit at our kitchen table as she filled a bowl with clean water. She sat beside him and started to bathe his wound.

"How did this happen?" she asked me. "And why have you brought a dog into our house?"

I told her about the strange red headed girl and the puppy while she put a large plaster over Antony's cut.

"Now just rest, Antony, dear. I'll fetch you a glass of water. Then I must tell your mother."

"She's out until five o'clock at her club."

Stella looked at her watch. "Well, it's a few minutes to five now, so I'll give her a knock."

She made sure Antony drank some water, then grabbed her door keys and went next door.

"Where's the dog, Annique?" Antony asked as he tried to get up.

"He's in the living room behind the sofa. Do you think Stella will let him stay?"

He shrugged. "Hopefully she'll take pity on him. But I wouldn't bet on it."

Stella returned with Kirsty, who looked horrified when she saw the large plaster on her son's head, and a bruise beginning to appear over his left eye.

"Let me get you home, Antony. You need to go straight to bed."

"Aw Mum, I don't need to go to bed. I'll be fine. Don't

fuss so much."

"No arguing, Antony - head wounds can be serious. You may have suffered concussion. You must rest for a while."

We waved them goodbye and I went into our living room.

"Come on little one," I coaxed.

Slowly the puppy slid out from behind the sofa and came towards me.

I stroked him and noticed he had a small lump behind his ear. He squealed when I parted the hair around it while trying to take a closer look.

"All right little boy, you've had some bad times I can tell, but I promise from now on things will be different."

I carried him into the kitchen where Stella was washing out the bowl she'd used to clean Antony's wound. She turned and said: "I still don't know why you've brought this dog into our home."

"He's so cute, Stella. I'd like to keep him."

"No, I'm afraid you can't."

I saw the red rim in her eyes. This was not going to be easy.

"Please," I pleaded.

"I haven't got time to waste talking about this dog. Now, for the time being, put him in the shed."

"But Stella, he'll be scared, especially when it gets dark..."

"You heard what I said, Annique - put him in the shed

right now."

Deciding not to argue with her, I opened the back door and carried the puppy to our den. At least it was full of comfy cushions and he soon chose a large orange one to curl up on.

"Okay, wait there and I'll get you something to eat."

I returned with a little dish containing two of the sausages that Stella had cooked earlier and a bowl filled with water. The puppy gobbled up the sausages and slurped all the water before returning to his cushion, spinning round a few times until he got comfortable and then licking his paws.

"You are a good boy," I said as he wagged his tail happily and rolled over to let me tickle his tummy. When he became sleepy I backed out of the shed, quietly closed the door and made my way to the house.

Returning fifteen minutes later, I was pleased to see the puppy was fast asleep. He was alright for now - but how would he cope if Stella made me get rid of him?

CHAPTER 21

Bright sunshine streaming through my window caused me to wake up early on my thirteenth birthday.

I dressed quickly and rushed to see if the puppy was alright. As soon as I entered the shed he jumped up and down around my legs. Then he spun around a few times and peed on the floor. I couldn't help laughing.

The little dog seemed pleased with himself and began to wag his tail non-stop. "Waggles - that's what I'll call you."

Returning to the house, I found Stella had set the kitchen table for six people and was cooking breakfast. Sausages, eggs and bacon all sizzled on the cooker.

"What a wonderful smell, Stella. Are we expecting visitors?"

"Yes. I thought I'd arrange a surprise for you - a birthday breakfast fry-up followed by pancakes. I've invited Antony and his parents."

"That's great. Thank you. It's a lovely idea."

Stella smiled and said "Happy birthday. You'll get your cards and presents when we are all sitting together for breakfast."

"Can I take a couple of sausages for Waggles?"

"Who?"

"That's what I've called the puppy because he wags his tail a lot. Don't you think it's a great name?"

Before Stella could reply the doorbell rang. She went to answer it, giving me the chance to put two sausages on a plate, fill a small bowl with water and take them to the den.

When I got back Antony, Kirsty and Lee were gathered in the lounge and burst into a loud chorus of 'Happy Birthday'.

Antony still had a plaster covering his forehead.

"How's the walking wounded?" I asked.

"I'm fine, thanks, Kidda. Never been..."

Kirsty interrupted him. "What my son means is that his wound was treated by a doctor at Accident and Emergency last night and it is not too serious."

She then handed me a gift bag. "We popped into a supermarket on the way back from the hospital and thought you might need these."

I looked inside and found a red dog collar and matching lead. Surely Stella and Graham would let me keep my new pet now.

"Thank you so much. Waggles will look very smart in these."

"So you've named him already."

"Yes, his tail never stops wagging - it's the perfect name."

We all sat round the kitchen table, chatting and laughing between mouthfuls. I managed to look at my cards before the second course of pancakes, and then excitedly opened my other presents.

Stella and Graham had bought me books, clothes - most of which I would never have chosen myself - a pair of shoes and the mascara I'd asked for. There was no sign of the mobile phone I'd requested. I was thirteen and didn't have a phone yet!

Antony cheered me up by suddenly producing a small box, with a picture of a rose on the front, and thrusting it into my hands. Inside was a silver pendant with 'Annique' on it. I thanked him, planted a kiss on his cheek, and put the chain around my neck.

Stella began to collect the dishes. I stood up to help, but Graham told me: "We'll see to those. You'd better go and take care of the dog, but keep him in the shed."

"I think you mean the den, Graham."

He gave me one of his stern stares, but, before he could speak, Antony said: "I'll come with you, Annique."

I grabbed the red dog collar and lead and marched out of the room, followed by Antony. As we made our way to the den he asked: "Would you like some chocolates?" and produced a box of Quality Street that he had been hiding behind his back.

"Hmm, thanks. I might give you a couple if you ask nicely." We both choose hazelnut.

When I opened the door of the den Waggles flashed past us and tore round the garden before cocking his leg up against a lavender bush.

"Waggles! No!" I shouted, shooing him away from Stella's favourite shrub. He then pooed in a flower bed of roses and, set off again, scampering around the garden three more times as if an express train was chasing him. Finally the excited puppy flopped down, exhausted.

"Oh, you really are a cute fellow, aren't you?" I told the wriggling little bundle at my feet as Antony helped me put the collar on him.

We then found a trowel to bury the offending poo. While we were doing so Stella came out of the back door but I managed to keep her talking while Antony finished the clean-up operation without her noticing.

CHAPTER 22

Our visitors went home around mid-day and soon afterwards the phone rang.

Stella answered it and seemed agitated while having a short, garbled conversation with whoever was calling. "Yes, I understand," she said before putting down the phone and shouting:

"Graham, Graham. They're coming for us today. Turn on your bracelet - they want to give you some instructions."

Who's coming, Stella?" I asked. "Are we having more guests for my birthday?"

She didn't answer as she rushed up the stairs into Graham's office, slamming the door behind her. A few minutes later she returned and called me into the living room.

"Now, Annique, I don't want you to ask any of your usual questions - just listen to me.

Please go up to your bedroom and pack some warm clothes. We're going on a trip."

"What! Where?"

"I told you not to ask questions - I haven't got time to answer them. Just put as many clothes as you can get in a suitcase, please."

"But how can I know what I'll need, Stella? You're scaring me."

"Sorry," she said in a rare apology. "We're going on a surprise holiday. Just think of it as another birthday surprise."

It all sounded most strange, but I did as she instructed, stuffing as many clothes as I could get into my blue case for a trip to goodness knows where. I crammed Baggins and Little Stella in among my clothes and toiletries, and put on my special bracelet and locket as well as my new pendant.

When I emerged from my bedroom I saw Graham carrying a much larger suitcase and a briefcase into the hall.

"Can we take Waggles with us?" I asked.

"That's not possible, Annique," he replied, raising his bushy eyebrows in disapproval.

"I'll ask Antony to look after him, then."

"No, you can't do that. Antony and his parents are coming with us."

I burst into tears and ran out to the den where I lifted Waggles off another wet cushion and hugged him. My heart was pounding. There was no way I was going to leave him - I'd refuse to go!

But first I must try one more time to get Graham and Stella to change their minds.

Carrying Waggles into the lounge, I was immediately confronted by Graham. He ran his right hand over his bald head and snapped: "Annique, I told you that we can't take that dog. Give him to me."

"Please, please Graham, let me take him with us."

Stella came into the room and, through my tears, I pleaded with her instead. "Please Stella, please let me have him. He's an abandoned baby and no one wants him. You can't just throw him out. Surely you can see he's only little and needs a family. Everyone needs a family, Stella. Can you imagine how it must feel to have lost your parents, and nobody loves you."

She looked at Graham. Perhaps something I had said was making them have second thoughts. Maybe calling Waggles an abandoned baby had done the trick.

I desperately tried to keep Waggles still. It would be disastrous if he misbehaved at this crucial moment. I prayed he wouldn't pee on the carpet. Finally Graham shrugged and left the room. He was apparently leaving the final decision to Stella.

"Yes, all right, stop going on," she said. "We'll take the animal with us. But you will have to be responsible for keeping him under control, Annique."

"Thank you, thank you, Stella. I love you so much." I put him down and went across to give her a kiss on the cheek, followed by a big hug.

"Annique, pull yourself together child," she said, pushing me gently away.

Stella had odd little ways, and affection embarrassed her, but that didn't mean she was a bad person. She had allowed me to have my own dog - nothing else could be as good as that.

"Now I must get ready," Stella informed me. "We are going on a long journey with Antony and his family."

"But where to?"

"Soon everything will be revealed to you, child."

*****

I bent down to stroke Waggles and he wriggled his way into my arms, giving me several licks and slobbery kisses.

"You're the best present ever," I told him, stroking his floppy little ears. I'd always wanted a dog of my own - a pal, someone I could talk to and tell all my troubles without being criticised.

"This is going to be the start of a wonderful friendship, Waggles. We can both keep each other company wherever we end up."

But I needed to know what was going on - and my best human friend, Old Boot Antony, was the ideal person to tell me.

When I got back to my bedroom I put Waggles down and used the bracelet Antony had given me to contact him.

"Antony, it's me, hello... are you there."

The mechanism on the bracelet whirled around and his face appeared on the screen.

"Antony, I can see you."

"Yeah, me, too, I mean I can see you. What's up?"

"Stella is being really mysterious. She says we're going away and that you're coming as well. Where are we going?"

"I can't tell you, Annique. My parents say that your dad is going to explain everything when we come round later. So you're just going to have to wait a little longer, Kidda. See you soon."

With that he cut off the connection.

'He knows where we're going, I'm sure of it,' I thought as the bracelet stopped whirling.

CHAPTER 23

At 3pm the doorbell rang. It was Antony and his parents, who Stella ushered into the lounge. They all looked rather glum. There was no sign of Antony's usual soppy grin and he wasn't even chewing gum! This must be serious.

I'd been allowed to let Waggles stay in the house and he lay between my feet on the deep pile of our red carpet as I sat on our sofa between Kirsty and Stella. Antony and his Dad Lee were seated on stiff backed chairs.

Graham came in and stood by our old oak bookcase. He, like Lee, was wearing a grey tunic and black trousers that I'd never seen them in before.

Stella suddenly took hold of my hand and held it tightly, which was very unusual for her. It made me apprehensive. I had an awful feeling as I gazed across at Antony, who smiled sheepishly and then avoided making eye contact with me by staring down at the carpet.

Before Graham could speak, Stella squeezed my hand again and said: "Annique, what we are about to tell you will come as a shock, but we all want you to know that whatever happens from this moment, you will always have our support."

Clearing his throat, Graham began talking. "You

remember when we spoke about your powers, Annique, we told you that if certain people found out they might try to take you away from us?"

"Yes," I replied, wondering what was coming next.

"Well, the risk of that happening has increased. We can't remain here any longer. In fact, we will all be leaving tonight, Annique."

"Are we leaving for good?" I asked. "Where will we go?"

"We're going home to our planet Thaasia."

I was dumbfounded as Graham continued: "It must sound incredible to you, but your real mother and father, King Daald and Queen Lalia, were rulers of Thaasia and that is where we all come from."

It hit me like a bombshell and I began to shake.

"What do you mean, my mother and father? You're my parents," I cried, looking from Graham to Stella in alarm.

"No," Graham said. "We are not your parents - we are your humanoid guardians. You are Princess Annaaqualalia Anastasia, of the royal house of Thaasia. And you should be our Queen."

Another Bombshell! It felt as if my brain would explode with all this startling information.

"I don't believe it," I shouted at Graham. "I'm not going anywhere." I jumped up and rushed out of the room in a state of panic.

Wrenching open the back door, I ran out into the den. Waggles bounded after me, barking and yelping, presumably thinking it was a game of chase.

As I stood crying, a pair of strong arms encircled me. "Don't worry," whispered Antony. "I'll be with you - you won't be doing this on your own."

Recovering slightly, I asked: "Did you know about any of this, Antony?"

"Some of it. That holiday we went on - it wasn't to America. My parents took me to this other planet, Thaasia. It was a mind-blowing experience. That's why I was acting so strange when I got back. I hated not being able to tell you but they made me promise that I wouldn't."

"So your parents are from this other planet as well?"

"Yes. I am, too. We all are. I couldn't believe it at first. I know how you must be feeling now."

"Does that mean you and your parents are humanoids as well?"

"No, we're Thaasians like you."

"But why did your parents take you back there?"

"They wanted to see if it was safe for you to return. As Graham said, you are a Princess, and my parents, like Graham and Stella, are very concerned for your safety. Look, we'd better go back inside, Annique - you need to be told the rest."

"Oh, Antony... Annique's not even my real name. I'm not the person I thought I was. How will I be able to cope with all this? I can't do it, Antony...I can't."

"Don't worry," he tried to reassure me. "I'll always protect you - with my life if necessary."

I remembered how he looked when we first met, skinny with freckles. He'd become a young man. I felt a wave of love for him as he promised to protect me.

"We have to go back, Annique. You'll have to be braver than you've ever been before, but always remember I will be by your side - that's my job now."

"What do you mean?"

"That's what I have to do - always be there for you."

"Always?"

"Well nearly always." He smiled, looking a bit embarrassed.

I suddenly realised that I might be better equipped to protect Antony than him look after me if I still had my powers on this strange place they wanted to take me.

CHAPTER 24

"This has obviously come as a huge shock to you, Annique," said Kirsty sympathetically when Antony and I, hand in hand, followed by Waggles, rejoined her and the other adults in the lounge. "I know Antony could not take it all in at first. You were both born on Thaasia, but came here as babies and have spent almost all your lives on Earth so no wonder if seems unbelievable to you."

Stella flashed me one of her rare smiles. "We wanted to break it to you more gently, but we could not risk you telling anyone. That's why we have left it until the day of departure."

"So I was named after my... real mother."

"That's right," Graham confirmed. He seemed to have a look of disapproval on his face, but I could not tell if this was because I was holding Antony's hand, as I stood next to him, or the fact that Waggles was scratching himself while sitting on the carpet.

"Why aren't I with my parents, then? If they are from another planet why am I living here on Earth with you and Stella?"

"Your parents are...dead," Graham replied. "They were killed by your uncle, Prince Kaarn, who is now the king of Thaasia."

Antony squeezed my hand as I shouted out: "Why? Why did he do that?"

It was Antony's father Lee who answered. "Because Kaarn is a very greedy, power-crazy, evil person. And he is completely ruthless."

I couldn't keep quiet. Questions needed answering, and my head was full of them. "What about my grandparents? Are they still alive?"

"Unfortunately not," said Stella. "But they passed on their powers to your Mother and she, in turn, passed them on to you. They originally came from the planet Riola. Nobody else on Thaasia has those powers."

"Why am I going back now? Why have you waited until I'm thirteen?"

Graham told me: "We have to go now. We think our enemies have found out where you are?"

"I don't want to go, Graham. I've been brought up on Earth, and I feel human. I don't even know what is expected of me."

Graham looked agitated as he went on: "As we've told you, your uncle now rules Thaasia, but he is not the true heir to the throne - you are. At the age of thirteen you are old enough to return home and become Queen."

A picture *flashed* through my mind of Queen Boudica on her horse-drawn chariot, chasing off the evil Kaarn and his men - only she had my face. 'Well, that's not going to happen', I thought, 'especially as Boudica was beaten by the Romans'. I've never been a particularly brave person, and the sight of blood always makes me feel queasy. Some warrior Queen I'd make!

"How did my parents die?" I asked, wanting to know the awful truth.

Graham continued: "It happened at your 'Naming Ceremony'. On our planet the King and Queen's first child officially becomes recognised as an heir to the throne on their second somara."

"What's a somara?"

"They are called years here. It was your second somara - your second birthday. A huge banquet was held in your honour and King Daald carried you into the Great Hall where hundreds..."

Stella interrupted: "I can still vividly remember how the hall was covered in red and gold garlands and bunting. As custom dictates, you were held above your father's head and he called out your name to everybody. 'Annaaqualalia Anastasia". Everyone cheered. We were all so proud."

A loud sob came from the sofa as Kirsty put her hands over her face.

Graham took up the story. "The King acclaimed you. It meant that you were being officially confirmed as the next in line to the throne. When the ceremony was complete we all sat down for the feast that followed."

Stella again cut in. "I remember the delicious smell as hundreds of roast Arrks were brought in for the banquet. They are similar to oxen, but even bigger. There was dish upon dish of wonderful food, and the hall was full of joyful people. I had never seen the King and Queen look so happy."

She paused and seemed lost in the memory for a few moments before adding: "Wine was poured into silver goblets and the King made a toast 'To Princess Annaqualalia'.

"Goblets were raised and red wine drank. But within seconds the echoes of laughter turned to gurgles and screams as everyone held their throats, collapsing around the hall in agony. Every bottle had been poisoned."

Graham explained: "It was awful. Stella and I do not drink alcohol so we survived. We saw everything. I was standing on guard behind the King and Queen but could do nothing to save them.

"The Queen had been holding you in her arms when she toppled forward. She handed you to Stella as she tried to stagger to her feet and her crown fell from her head. The King reached out to her and they died in each other's arms."

My legs felt weak and I slumped against Antony, who supported me. Even my nightmares were not as bad as the reality.

Kirsty raised her head as Lee added: "We were also on guard duty that day and did not drink the poisoned wine, either. The four of us escaped with you and Antony. We fled to Earth, a planet our scientists had told us was most like our own, and made our homes here."

"Yes," said Graham. "I sent our spaceship back into orbit. If anyone on Earth spotted it they would have thought it was an unidentified flying object. We split up to lessen the risk of being detected. So Antony and his parents went to Swindon until it was considered safe for them to join us here in Surrey. You and Antony were too young to remember what had happened and it seemed best to let you believe you had been born on Earth.

"Kaarn and his men had no idea where we were - that is until now. Our loyal friends from Thaasia have informed us that Kaarn has sent several agents to Earth and it would be only a matter of time before they found us. We must go back to Thaasia and join forces with those plotting to overthrow him."

CHAPTER 25

As I stood in the kitchen ten minutes later, Stella was cramming a pair of shoes into a haversack that already seemed full to bursting point.

"Thank you for saving my life and taking care of me all these years, Stella," I blurted out, laying my hand gently on her shoulder. I'm so pleased you and Graham adopted me."

"That's not strictly true, Annique. It was our duty to look after you and we were delighted to do so. Humanoids, like us, were known for our superior strength and so we became protectors to the Thaasian people.

"Every humanoid was given some genes of the person he or she was assigned to. We were lucky enough to be assigned to your father and mother. It was an honour to serve them, and then to be appointed your protectors.

"When your uncle killed your parents and most of those at the banquet, our first thought was to get you away to safety. Since then Graham and I have seen it as our duty to look after you. I hope when you become Queen we can still be of service." Stella stood tall and proud beside me as she spoke.

I was seeing a new side to Stella - not the one I knew

as a mother-figure in a frilly pink apron.

"If I do become Queen, I will always want you and Graham with me, not just as my protectors, but as my family and friends." Despite what they'd told me, I still regarded them as my parents - even if they lacked most of the emotions shown by humans. I loved them.

"Thank you Annique. First we must topple Kaarn. It won't be easy, but he is hated by so many people on Thaasia that many of them have formed a secret rebel army. They will help us to overcome him and enable you to take over the throne."

CHAPTER 26

A few hours later we prepared to leave the little semi-detached home I'd lived in for most of my life.

"Hurry up Annique," shouted Stella as I did one final rummage through the drawers in my bedroom.

'Why hadn't they told me just a little sooner and given me more time to prepare?' I'd filled a suit case and was now stuffing a back-pack with things I believed I could not live without, including photos and a tiny music box I'd been given for my fifth birthday.

Stella hadn't seemed to notice Waggles sneak into my room. He sat on the bed with his head resting between his paws, not taking his eyes off me. He didn't look happy. I went over and gave him a stroke, forgetting about the sore behind his ear. As I touched the lump he yelped in pain.

"What's the matter with your ear, Waggles? I wish we had time to take you to the vets so that he could have a look." I gently lifted him off the bed and put him on the floor, then picked up my bag and suitcase before pausing to take one last look at my little bedroom. Even the hated photo of Fizz and her friends seemed to evoke sentimental feelings in me. I took it out of its frame and slipped it in my bag.

Once downstairs, I dropped everything in the hall. Just one more thing I had to do before I left forever. With Waggles running after me, I went out into the back garden and stood looking at the den. The old sign **'KEEP OUT - SECRET DEN - ENTER AT YOUR PERIL'** was the worse for wear. As I ran my fingers over it, I could remember Antony's words from all those years ago when we first met: "How about us playing with your exploding light ball?"

I opened the den door. All our things were inside - the cushions which Antony and I still occasionally threw at each other, books and comics, the posters on the walls. Another memory came into my mind of the day I first revealed to Antony I had *powers*. I smiled at the thought of him staring in disbelief.

Walking over to a pile of books, I quickly chose two of my favourites to take with me - Harry Potter and the Philosopher's Stone and Beauty and the Beast. Two books about people who had suddenly found their lives change forever - ironic, eh?

With Waggles under my arm, I ran my fingers over the den's door as I came out of it for the last time. Upon turning, I saw Antony standing at the kitchen door, taking a photo of our beloved den.

Thirty minutes later we all climbed into a large, black, 'presidential' type of car I'd never seen before.

Waggles, looking smart in his new red collar, and I squeezed into the back alongside Antony, Stella, Kirsty and

Lee, while Graham sat in front next to the driver, a stranger with a crescent shaped scar around his left eye.

As he started the engine and drove away, I turned to peer out of the back window for a final look at the little house I'd lived in since I was two years old. It became smaller and smaller until it disappeared from my view. All this would be gone forever. Tears started to run down my cheeks.

When we passed the stables, I blurted out: "Bella - I haven't said goodbye to Bella."

Antony squeezed my arm as I sobbed: "Do you think the horses will miss us?"

"They're bound to," he comforted. "But they'll be alright. Nobody could look after them better than Beryl and her stable lad Steve."

I'd loved riding Bella because of her calm and loving nature - not like Crispin, Antony's fiery steed.

While the car sped on, I turned to look at Antony, and he, too, seemed very sad. In my grief I'd forgotten that he was leaving his home, too. It was selfish of me not to realise sooner. How was he going to cope?

The enormity of it all suddenly hit me. We were leaving our homes, our schools, our friends, our horses - and our planet. It was too much to take in and I buried my head in Waggles' soft fur while shedding more tears.

"Don't cry," Antony said, soothingly.

"Will I be able to contact my friends?" I asked.

"That's very unlikely, Kidda."

"Emma and Jennifer will wonder what has happened to me. And what about my school? Won't they report me missing?"

"Hopefully not," said Stella. "I've put a letter in the post to them, explaining that we've had to leave at short notice. I couldn't tell the headmistress the real reason so I said we're going to the aid of family members involved in a tragedy abroad."

I suddenly felt so angry. "Stella, why wasn't I told about all this sooner? You could have trusted me."

"We had intended to prepare you, Annique, but things happened so quickly and we've been forced to leave earlier than we planned."

"What things?"

"Things like they found out where we were," interrupted Antony.

"Who found us?

Graham provided the answer. "As I explained to you earlier, Annique, we learned that Kaarn had sent his agents here to search for us."

"But what could they have done?" I demanded.

"They could have killed us," Antony said. "From what Dad has told me, Kaarn would have gone to any lengths to stop you returning as Queen."

"That's enough, Antony." Lee's stern voice silenced his son.

But Graham went on: "Antony is right. Our enemies have been trying to find us for years.

Now that they are closing in we must get to our ship as soon as possible."

"Our ship? Are we going by sea?"

Antony laughed loudly so I poked him in the ribs.

"What are you laughing at? It's not funny at all, is it?"

"Sorry, Annique," he apologised. "We are not travelling by that sort of ship - we're going on the long journey back to Thaasia by spaceship."

I sat in total silence the rest of the way, trying to stop my heart from racing, my stomach from churning and my head from pounding. The thought of travelling in a spaceship frightened me - I'd not even flown on a plane! And the prospect of taking on the dreaded Kaarn was even more terrifying.

At least Antony had been prepared for all this and given some advance warning. I was completely overwhelmed and my brain would not function properly.

My head became filled with all sorts of silly thoughts. Going to this far off planet meant I wouldn't be able to watch my favourite TV programmes. And what about all the latest music? Did these people on Thaasia even have television and music?

Another thought struck me and I started to feel guilty. What an awful, shallow person I really was. At a time like this, with people risking their lives, I was thinking about TV programmes and CDs. But wasn't that sort of thing what most young girls filled their heads with?

Dear Stella and Graham! This efficient, well organised

pair may have been a bit odd at times, but they'd looked after me so well. For thirteen years I'd not once feared that someone was planning to kill me. All this time Stella and Graham had been watching and protecting me. This explained Graham's iron control, which occasionally I'd rebelled against, and Stella's obsessive behaviour. It also accounted for their reluctance to let me bring friends back home, or go out with them, when I was younger. The weight of protecting the Princess of Thaasia - *me* - had fallen on their shoulders.

As I sat in the car cuddling Waggles, I promised myself that if we survived I would repay them, somehow.

CHAPTER 27

We travelled for about two hours in the rain before turning off down a very narrow, bumpy lane, and finally stopping at a wooden gate. The driver opened it and then drove across a wet, muddy field.

When we came to an abrupt halt I pulled Waggles closer to me as the rain beat against the car windows and a mist started to engulf us.

"Stay here," Graham said, getting out of the car. He began walking through the thick grass and disappeared in the mist.

"Where's Graham gone!?" I shouted in alarm. "He's just vanished."

"It's okay," Kirsty assured me. "He'll be back soon."

Waggles started to fidget and whine.

"I think he wants a wee, Stella."

She sighed and got out of the car. Taking him from me, with his lead attached, she put the dog on the grass. He sniffed around for some seconds before relieving himself.

"Good boy," I said as he jumped back onto my lap, the wet from his paws seeping through my jeans. He gave me a slobbery lick.

"Now your jeans are all muddy, Annique," scolded

Stella. "How could we have been foolish enough to bring a messy dog with us? Give him to me."

"No, Stella, no way." I held on to Waggles tightly, refusing to let her have him.

Graham materialised from out of nowhere, and waved to us. It was just the distraction needed to save Waggles because I was sure Stella had intended to abandon him in the field.

Butterflies were dancing around inside my stomach as we all got out of the car and walked towards Graham. I took some deep breaths to calm my nerves, but the butterflies turned into stampeding buffaloes, and when I lost sight of Graham and Stella, I found it hard to move. Even the normally fun loving Waggles was growling in alarm and pulling back on the end of his lead. I put my hand on my right wrist, checking to see if I still had my bracelet on. It was there, but it didn't calm my nerves.

Fortunately Antony waited for me to catch him up. "I don't like this - I really don't," I told him. "My legs have turned to jelly."

Antony gently guided me forward, through the haze, and then I saw it. Out of nowhere a huge space ship materialised. It was enormous and hovered silently over the ground. My mouth fell open in astonishment and I grabbed Antony's arm. "Good grief," I gasped. "Look at the size of it."

The silver craft had a red crest on the side with some kind of creature in full flight painted on it. And along the length were a mass of windows.

Graham and Stella came up to stand beside us. "Close your eyes, Annique," Graham said firmly. Not wanting to have any more shocks, I did as he instructed without question, holding on tightly to Waggles.

A thousand little fingertips seemed to gently touch my whole body as I was lifted off my feet. Waggles went limp in my arms. I wanted to take a look, but I was too scared.

"It's okay, Annique, you can look now," Antony's voice floated towards me. I took a deep breath and opened one eye, fearing what I was about to see.

We were no longer standing in a damp, muddy field, but were inside the spacecraft.

Opening the other eye, I looked around at four grey metallic walls, but where was the door? No sooner had the thought entered my head than the walls became obscured by thousands of popping crystals. As each one burst and disappeared I could see we were in a large chamber.

A panel slid open and a stranger emerged, with long side whiskers that meant he had more hair on his face than on his balding head. He was dressed in a grey tunic and black trousers, like the ones Graham and Lee were wearing. He bowed his head before speaking to me. I recognised my new name, Annaaqualalia Anastasia, but could not understand the other words he was uttering.

Then it struck me, I was going to another planet where they wouldn't speak English.

"Put these in your ears," Stella told us, holding out

little gadgets to Antony and myself. I gave her a puzzled look, put Waggles down on the floor and did as she said. Antony had already inserted his device into his right ear - of course, he'd been to this planet before and knew what to expect.

The man in the uniform spoke again, and this time I could understand him.

Wow, they are clever on Thaasia. And I'm their Princess!

"My name is Chief Yuul Chaan, of your Imperial Army," the man said. "I welcome you on board my ship, your royal Saaena." Another strange word for me to get used to! The Chief continued: "Agent 319 will take you to your quarters." I frowned as he gestured towards Stella. "I trust that you have been well cared for on Earth by 319 and 320."

I was annoyed at the way he referred to Stella and Graham. They weren't numbers - they'd brought me up, kept me safe. For the first time I practised what would, I was sure, become second nature to me in time, my *Princess* voice.

Standing as tall as my 160cm would allow me, I attempted to exert my *authority*.

"Thank you for your kind welcome, Chief Chaan," I said. "319 will indeed accompany me to my quarters, but from now on she is to be known as Stella, and her companion will be called Graham. They are the names I've grown used to and I see no reason to change them."

I could see the look of surprise in Chaan's eyes, as I said this, and I heard Graham's sharp intake of breath. But Chaan bowed his head and assured me that he'd make it known aboard his ship.

Surely Stella and Graham would be pleased to be known by their Earth names. But I had my doubts as I looked at their stern faces, and then saw Graham pass his right hand over his bald head.

Had I done the wrong thing?

CHAPTER 28

After the brief introductions and my brave little speech, I was escorted along a brightly-lit corridor to my cabin.

Waggles pulled on his lead until we got to a door which swished open, causing him to cower behind me.

The cabin was luxurious and spacious, with white walls and shiny black tiles on the floor.

There was a very large bed, covered by a purple silk spread, two chairs and a small table. Six shelves along the wall on the right hand side contained a lot of small cubes, similar to children's building blocks. Every one of them had a different coloured face and strange writing.

I was trying to make out what they were when there was a knock on the door, and Stella entered, carrying my things. She'd changed into the same style of tunic as Graham and Lee.

"Stella, you look so different. Haven't you brought your pink apron with you?" As soon as the words came out I realised it was a mistake. "Sorry, Stella, it's just that I already miss the way things were at home. So what happens now?"

"We will take off very soon."

"Have the people who are looking for us got ships as

big as this one?"

"Yes. Kaarn has lots of them. But we should be safe. Just try to relax."

Turning to the shelves again, I picked up a bright red cube. Immediately the little face on it smiled and a mechanical voice spoke. I was still wearing my ear piece so I could understood what it was saying.

"Put on the glasses, state the language required and select a title."

"Er...English," I answered, slipping on a pair of glasses which were laying on one of the shelves. All the strange writing on the six-sided boxes immediately changed into English.

"Wow, that's amazing," I giggled.

The titles showed they contained all sorts of information about the spacecraft and Thaasia.

Before I could choose one, Waggles jumped on the bed, barking excitedly. He sniffed the pillow, growled and then began to tear it apart with his teeth.

"Stop that!" shouted Stella.

When Waggles looked round at her there was pillow stuffing all over his face and he was holding a small, strange metal object in his mouth. I was about to take it from him when Stella warned: "Don't touch that - it might be dangerous."

"What do you mean, dangerous?" I asked in alarm.

"Just do not touch it, Annique. I will have it examined." Stella gingerly removed the circular object from Waggles' mouth and put it in her pocket. Then she pulled back the bedclothes and looked over the bed thoroughly without finding any sign of other mysterious items.

"There does not appear to be anything else," she said, while checking out other parts of the cabin. "It's a good job the dog found that,"

"Clever boy, Waggles," I said, tickling him behind his ear. He backed away, whimpering, and I remembered the lump.

"Is that still sore, Waggles?" He looked at me with a pained expression and I held him close to let him know I cared. Waggles excitedly licked my hand, bouncing around again.

He was such a loving puppy. I found it hard to imagine how someone could hurt him – what kind of person would do that? He was so cute when he pricked up his ears or gave me a cheeky grin.

I sat cuddling Waggles as Stella walked to the door, holding the metal object he'd found. "I'll find out what this is and get you another pillow," she said.

After a few minutes I decided to unpack and as soon as I opened my case out tumbled my old teddy bear Baggins and my doll Little Stella. I hugged them to me, hoping they would help to prepare me for the ordeal ahead.

*****

Suddenly the spaceship's engines began roaring as we

lifted off the ground. It was so scary, but also exhilarating as we rose higher and higher with a whoosh. I rushed to the window in my cabin. The field was no longer visible and I could barely make out the surrounding countryside or any buildings as we swiftly soared into the sky.

How amazing that I'd never been further than Eastbourne before and now, here I was, in a spacecraft flying to another planet!

There'd been no chance to say goodbye to life on the world I'd known. As I peered through the window Earth became a ball that got smaller and smaller until it finally disappeared.

I began to doubt very much if I could be as brave as my parents, or Stella and Graham, convinced I was going to be a big disappointment to everyone when they got to know me.

Stella eventually returned to my cabin carrying a new pillow and I asked if the gadget she had taken was as dangerous as she had suspected.

"It was a bugging device," she revealed. "Chief Chaan is carrying out an investigation to find out who planted it in your pillow."

"Could it have been one of Kaarn's men? Is there a spy on board?"

"Maybe. Or it might have simply been put there by an over-cautious member of the crew."

"Where's Antony? Has he got a room near to ours?"

"He is two rooms away with his parents. Graham and I

are in the next room to you so stop worrying, Annique. You are safe with us all on hand to look after you."

"Is Thaasia very far away, Stella? How long is it going to take us to get there?"

"Our planet is in the Chosha galaxy, many light years away, but this ship is so fast the journey will only take a few days. Our craft are far more advanced than those on Earth. The Thaasian scientists have observed with amusement the endeavours of the Americans and Russians to travel in space."

"Won't people on Earth have spotted this ship?" I asked.

"No. We have been able to develop a cloaking device to make it invisible, and once we reach a certain height it can travel at speeds beyond light."

There was a knock at the door and Stella went to answer it. A young woman stood at the entrance with a large tray of food, some of which looked rather strange. That didn't seem to bother Waggles, who jumped off the bed, greedily licking his lips and wagging his tail.

Stella took the tray from the girl who then removed the mess Waggles had made of the old pillow, bowed to me and backed out of the door without saying a word.

The best way to describe the appearance of what I saw on the plates she had left us was lumpy dark green custard and loads of little red eyes in a bed of brown leaves.

"What is it, Stella?" I asked, not keen to try any of it.

"If you taste some you will be pleasantly surprised,

Annique. It is all quite delicious."

I took a couple of brown leaves and just one red eye. The leaves tasted like over-cooked sprouts (yuk) and I could not bring myself to put the 'eye' in my mouth. I threw it to Waggles, who greedily ate it before barking furiously and being sick next to the bed.

Stella shrieked. "Why, why, why did you bring this... awful creature with us? I shall put him in the hold until we arrive." With that she scooped him up into her arms.

"No Stella, you cannot do that. Sorry, but I am to be your Queen, and I want Waggles to stay with me. End of discussion."

Power is wonderful sometimes, you know.

She looked a bit shocked, but put Waggles down and then got a towel from the bathroom to clean the sick off the carpet.

I could see that familiar red rim beginning to glow in her eyes. I'd better be careful, I thought, Queen or no Queen.

"Thank you, Stella," I said hastily.

I tried a spoonful of the lumpy brown custard, which tasted a lot better- similar to peanut butter - and handed Waggles what looked like a biscuit. He sniffed it warily before eating it.

Now seemed the best time to approach the subject of Stella's and Graham's names.

"I hope you're pleased that I didn't want to call you and Graham by a number."

"We humanoids are not ashamed of our numbers. They show our priority on Thaasia.

Humanoids who have a number in the 300s are very highly thought of. The names Stella and Graham will mean nothing on Thaasia."

"But they mean something to *me*, Stella. You and Graham took over as my parents when I was a very young child, and I couldn't call you by numbers now."

Stella gave me a smile which was probably meant to be sympathetic even though it looked forced. "We are honoured you think of us that way, Annique, but would ask you to let us be referred to by our numbers when we are in public."

Oh dear, was this the first of many mistakes I'd make with the humanoids? I didn't know their ways - how was I going to cope trying to live with them on a different planet? I hoped Stella and Graham wouldn't change too much.

CHAPTER 29

Despite all my worries and fears, I had a good night's sleep and felt much better the next morning. Being served breakfast in bed helped!

My ear-piece would enable me to talk to anybody on the spaceship, and the cubes in my cabin meant I could find out more information. The little cubes projected a screen like a Kindle at home and I chose a book about the history of Thaasia.

I noted with interest that their scientists had invented a wonder pill that could feed all the people on Thaasia. It was very beneficial in some areas where the people had trouble growing food, or after natural disasters that could cause famine. But, given a choice, people preferred the natural taste of fish, meat and properly grown vegetables and fruit.

Waggles had settled down, too. We played together and ate together - and he got used to weeing in a tray in the bathroom. I offered to empty it, but Stella refused to let me.

"You will be the Queen of Thaasia," she reminded me. "It would not look right for you to be carrying a dog toilet down the corridor."

She picked up the offensive tray herself, holding her

nose and moaning: "As if things are not difficult enough, without having a smelly dog on board."

After she'd left, I gave Waggles a biscuit and praised him as he gobbled it down. "Who's a clever boy then? Who did a wee wee? And who loves his little tummy tickled?"

"Okay, you've guessed my guilty secret," said a voice behind me.

I spun round and there was Antony, leaning casually against the door frame just as he'd once done at our den door. He was even chewing gum!

"Hello Antony. Is this a social visit or have you come for a particular reason?" I asked in an attempt to take the silly grin off his face.

"Do I need a special reason, now that you're such an important person?" He removed the gum from his mouth and put it back in the wrapper he'd taken from his pocket.

"No, never," I assured him, regretting my silly remark. "Never, never, never. You're my best friend and we can tell each other anything. Please treat me the same as you did on Earth, just to keep me sane and make me laugh."

"That's fine," he said, coming over and planting a kiss on my cheek. "But when others are around we must watch how we act, or I could end up in lots of trouble."

"Okay, when we are in public you will have to bow and scrape every time you see me," I giggled.

Antony laughed, too. "Maybe bow, but scrapping is out of the question."

Waggles suddenly began yelping after having a scratch.

"Hello boy, what's up?" Antony said gently. He stroked the dog's head and tried to look at the lump behind his ear but Waggles backed away.

"I think I should take him down to the medic so that he can have a look, Annique. The swelling near his ear has been annoying him for ages, hasn't it?"

"Hmm," I pondered. "That may be a good idea. Stella said it was nothing to worry about, probably just an old wound. But it's not getting any better and is obviously proving painful."

Old Boot took out another piece of gum and popped it into his mouth. No sooner had he done so than Stella walked in carrying the clean disinfected tray. He stopped chewing but it was too late!

"Antony, I'm sure you have duties to perform somewhere else," she said, flashing him a stern look. "And please do not try to hide the gum from me." She held out her hand and waited until he took it from his mouth to give it to her.

Stella turned to me. "Really, Annique, surrounding yourself with a smelly dog and a young man who chews gum is not the ideal image for the future Queen of Thaasia."

I was shocked at how she was treating Antony so differently now that it had been revealed I was a Princess and he was one of my subjects. I'd have to talk to her about this when we were alone.

Giving her my fiercest glare, which admittedly was

tame compared to some of hers, I replied: "Antony is performing an important duty here. He has kindly offered to take Waggles to have the lump behind his ear checked." I picked up my dog and handed him over to a gob-smacked Old Boot.

"See you soon - be a good boy. I mean the dog, not you, Antony."

Antony held on tight as Waggles struggled to get back to me. It was a good job Stella didn't see me wink before she closed the door on them both.

"Antony is my best friend," I reminded her. "What other duties could he have? He's only a bit older than me, so he won't be expected to fight or anything like that, will he?"

She shrugged, leaving me racked with worry. I couldn't bear the thought of him getting hurt.

CHAPTER 30

Less than three hours later Stella came into my cabin to announce: "We are approaching Thaasia, Annique. We will soon be facing the most dangerous part of our journey. Kaarn's men could be everywhere."

I wanted to look at my 'home' planet as we began flying nearer to it, but our spaceship had to remain cloaked, and grey shutters covered all the windows so I couldn't see anything.

Stella explained: "We have got to get past Kaarn's radar system and land undetected. Then we can join up with the rebel army who will give you their full support."

Despite the looming danger, my mind was occupied with concern for my dog. "I wonder when Waggles will be brought back. He's been away a long time. Can you go and find out if any thing's wrong, Stella?"

"Alright, I will go and check for you." she said, turning towards the door. But before she could open it there was a massive explosion that rocked the whole spacecraft and sent us both tumbling.

*****

I don't remember what happened in the next few

seconds because I hit my head as I fell and was momentarily knocked out. When I came round I heard terrible screams, followed by another explosion.

Sirens started wailing. I looked around and saw Stella laying on the floor, with part of the entrance door to my cabin having fallen on top of her. Lee, Kirsty and Antony came running up and managed to lift the door sufficiently to pull Stella clear of it.

Antony, who had blood trickling down his face from the old cut that had reopened on his forehead, and his mother came over to check on me.

"I'm OK," I assured them, although I was feeling rather groggy. "Don't worry about me - please look after Stella."

Lee gently lifted her into a sitting position and I could see that her left arm was hanging at an awkward angle. "I think your arm's broken," I murmured.

"I will be alright," Stella said unconvincingly.

Within seconds Graham appeared, his shirt ripped, and a wire sticking out of his neck, which really freaked me out. It brought home the fact that he was not really human.

"Graham - your neck..." I shouted over the noise as I got up gingerly.

"Never mind that - follow me quickly," he ordered.

"But what about Waggles?"

"I'll go back for him," said Antony. "I'll catch you up."

We followed Graham along the corridor. Ahead of us two members of the crew were bent over an injured colleague who was covered in blood and had a hole in his chest. His face was grey and his eyes seemed to stare blankly towards the ceiling.

Lee stopped and tried to help him, only to be told: "It's no good - he's dead."

"Please, please dear God, let us escape from this," I cried out.

We hurried past more crew members, through two sliding doors which swished open.

Graham led us down some steps and into a section containing five mini space ships that looked like wasps because they had yellow and black stripes on the sides.

Graham opened the door of the nearest wasp and told us to climb inside. Lee seated himself at the controls and flicked some switches, which caused the engine to rev up.

Seconds later a large hatch in the main spaceship slowly opened in front of us, revealing the vast, dark sky, dotted with sparkling stars.

"Buckle up quickly, Annique," said Kirsty as she sat beside me. I suddenly became aware that Stella was not on board. I looked out of the tiny window beside me and saw her picking herself up from the ground where she'd obviously stumbled.

"Wait!" I yelled. "Stella's still outside - and we can't go without Antony and Waggles."

"Take off - that's an order," Graham told Lee. "Antony and the dog can get in the next mini-ship with Stella."

"No!" I screamed and threw myself out of my seat

towards the door, pressing the button so that it swished open.

"Stella, get in," I shouted, frantically waving at her. She hastily flung herself through the door on to the floor of the small craft, gasping for breath and holding her injured arm.

"Let's wait for Antony and Waggles," I begged.

"We must go now," bellowed Graham. "If we don't take off immediately we could be caught in all the explosions."

"Please let's give them a few more minutes," I implored. But another violent eruption sounded almost on top of us.

Graham got up from his seat, looking as if he was about to grab the controls away from Lee.

"Take off, take off," he ordered. "We must save our future Queen."

Lee finally did so and the wasp hurtled through the open hatch into the darkness outside at break-neck speed.

I frantically used my bracelet to try to contact Antony and was so relieved when it lit up to show him on the tiny screen. He responded to my call and shouted "It's okay, Annique, I'm about to board...." but the connection was broken as we soared away from the main ship.

"I think Antony has made it to the wasps. I saw him on my bracelet."

"Thank goodness for that," Kirsty replied. "Who knows, his ship may stand a better chance of getting safely to Thaasia than us."

"How's your arm?" I asked Stella, who was sitting behind us.

"It's not too bad."

"And what about you, Graham?"

"Don't worry about us," he assured me. "Remember that Stella and I are humanoids so we can get our injuries repaired."

"What happened exactly?" I asked.

"Kaarn must have sent his own fleet of spaceships to attack us," Stella replied. "We were obviously betrayed. I had a suspicion that the gadget your dog found in your pillow was a bugging device planted by a treacherous member of our own crew."

"Dear Waggles. I do hope Antony has managed to rescue him."

Stella gave me a withering look, as if to say: 'at a time like this how can you think of a dog?'

CHAPTER 31

Kirsty and I stared out of the porthole windows in horror as missiles were being fired all around us.

"This is awful," I yelled, putting my hands over my ears to dull the noise of the blasts.

The spaceship that had brought us here was now ablaze, but those left on board it were bravely returning fire and one of Kaarn's ships suddenly exploded.

A terrible battle continued to be fought as Lee frantically swerved our wasp from side to side in an attempt to avoid a missile that was hurtling towards us.

"We're going to be blown to bits!" I shouted in panic.

My whole body began shaking uncontrollably as the missile missed us by inches and whooshed past my window.

"Annique, Annique," Kirsty's voice penetrated the turmoil inside my brain and made me focus on something familiar. "Annique, it is alright - we are here with you. Just breathe deeply."

A series of big breaths - and Kirsty's comforting tones - eventually calmed me down.

"We've made it," she said.

As I peered out of the wasp's window, I could make out the strange multi-coloured terrain of Thaasia below us.

When we came nearer I could see that the soil was tinged with a red hue and there were rivers covered in what appeared to be large orange water lilies.

Kirsty smiled at me reassuringly. "We were lucky to escape," she said. "Let us hope that Antony has got away, too."

'And Waggles', I thought.

CHAPTER 32

Our little ship flew low over a desert, with no visible vegetation in sight. Stella told me it was called Yaarim.

By sunset everything looked like a beautiful water canvas, with brush strokes of black, crimson and magenta streaking through the sky. In the distance, above a range of mountains, I could see the large shimmering moon. It was purple, identical to the one in my dreams, and it sent purple rays cascading over every rock.

Craning my neck to get a better view from the small window, I spotted a sizeable crater in the sand below.

"What's that?" I asked, as we flew lower and hovered over it. I could feel my stomach churning like mad.

"Don't worry," said Graham. "We've finally arrived and will be with friends."

Our craft glided into the crater, with huge doors opening to admit us and then closing over us. To my amazement we were in a massive, well equipped landing bay. At least fifty ships, exactly like the large one we'd flown on from Earth, were waiting in lines as far as my eyes could see.

I had been expecting the rebel army to be housed in a ramshackle old building – certainly nothing as grand or as big as this!

We touched down and Lee was the first to step out of our wasp. Graham followed, with Stella just behind, and finally me and Kirsty.

I saw that another mini-ship had just landed and six people were getting out of it. But there was no sign of Antony or Waggles.

Kirsty sighed and there were tears glistening in her eyes. Putting my arm around her shoulders, I tried to comfort her.

"Antony will be with us soon. He's going to be safe." I hoped with all my heart that I'd be proved right.

I tried using my communicator again, but the dial just kept spinning and could not make contact.

CHAPTER 33

We were welcomed by a tall, blond-haired man who introduced himself as Commander Saalim Geddaall, the head of the rebel army assembled in this secret domain. He bowed to me and said: "It is an honour to meet you Princess."

Despite the language device in my ear, I found it harder to understand his deep voice than I had the Thaasians on the spaceship.

I swallowed hard and could only mutter: "It's a pleasure to meet you, too."

The commander told us that our spaceship had been destroyed but that most of the crew had fled in mini craft like ours and he hoped they would also arrive safely.

My anxiety took over. "Were my friend Antony and my dog Waggles on the wasps?" I asked him.

"Wasps?"

"I mean the mini-ships."

"I am sorry, Princess, but I do not have that information at this time. We dispatched more space craft to do battle with those sent by Kaarn to attack the ship in which you had been travelling. There has been much fighting, but hopefully all the wasps, as you call them, will get through"

Commander Geddaall escorted us to our quarters, and I was given a luxurious room with a king-sized bed. I flopped on to it, exhausted.

After a few minutes there was a knock on the door and Stella came in. I immediately saw that her arm was still hanging limply by her side.

"Oh, Stella, your poor arm."

"Don't worry - I will get it fixed later," she said as if it was nothing. "Graham is having his neck repaired first and then I will get my arm replaced."

"You are so brave, Stella."

"I am just doing my duty. We are now safe with members of the rebel army in their underground headquarters. They are all pledged to serve you."

"That's great, but I just can't take it all in. A few days ago I was so happy riding my horse Bella and chasing after Antony."

"Try to accept that you are our Princess. Rest now - I'll return later." And she was gone.

Laying on the enormous bed, I reflected how Stella and Graham had been chosen to protect me. Maybe they were not even married. That would explain why I had never seen them holding hands or having a cuddle. After all, they were humanoids not humans. Stella had usually kept herself busy cleaning everything over and over again, while Graham had spent most of the time in his room working on his computer. They had seldom done things together. and

Graham rarely went out with us.

The more I thought about it the more I realised how little I'd seen of Graham over the years - it was usually Stella I went to for anything I needed. I had assumed he'd been busy working as an accountant, but he must have been in contact with Thaasia, planning our eventual return.

How strange it all was. I'd always thought of Stella and Graham as Mum and Dad, but they were humanoids numbers 319 and 320.

*****

For the first time I started to miss my real parents, and wondered what life with them would have been like. The woman who I'd always thought of as my grandmother, and who held me as a baby looking up at the purple moon, was actually my real mother. The one I dreamed about. My nightmares must have been prompted by the terrible way my parents were taken from me.

It was like jigsaw puzzle pieces falling into place. How many more missing pieces were there to find? How many more humanoids were there on Thaasia, and did any serve my Uncle Kaarn? That was a terrifying thought. I needed to know the answers to these questions.

There was another knock on the door. "Come in," I called automatically.

It opened, and standing there with a grin on his face was Antony.

I rushed over, flung my arms around him and planted a

big kiss on his cheek. "Thank goodness you're safe."

He kissed me back, then pulled away. "Sorry, I shouldn't have done that."

"Why not?"

"Because you're a princess and soon you'll be our queen."

"Don't be daft," I told him. "There's no need to treat me any differently. I'm so thankful you escaped. The bracelet allowed me to see you running towards the wasps in the hold, but then it went blank."

"A lot of the crew escaped with me. But I believe Chief Chaan remained on the spaceship, firing back at the enemy until the end."

"What about Waggles? Did you bring him with you?"

"No, but the medical staff did. They'd put him under sedation and refused to let me take him."

"Did they escape from the spaceship?"

"We don't know yet. Their mini-ship left after ours and has still to arrive."

*****

When Antony and I joined the others for lunch in a private suite I was relieved to see that Stella and Graham looked their old selves. Their injuries had obviously been repaired.

"Are you both OK, now?" I asked them.

"Yes, and I have been given a new hand, too," Stella said proudly. She demonstrated by rotating her left hand over and over again, first forwards and then backwards.

"Oh, that's really weird, Stella."

"Weird?"

"Yes, but in a good way," I lied.

As we sat at a round table together, eating some sort of thick brown stew, Lee told us that all but one of the wasps had landed at the base so far - the missing one was that carrying the medical staff and Waggles.

"It's too early to come to any conclusions," Lee added. "It was the last craft to leave the spaceship and so it is bound to be the last to arrive."

Antony seemed to sense my concern." Don't worry. I'm sure Waggles will be with us soon."

"I can't stop worrying. And I have so many questions rolling around in my head. It must have been the same when you came to Thaasia previously, Antony."

"You're right. It was such a shock. Until then I'd no reason to doubt that I was Antony Wellington from Swindon - I didn't for one moment suspect that I might have come from anywhere other than England."

"So what's your real name?"

"I'm not telling you."

"Why?"

"Because you'd laugh."

"No I won't. I promise. Is it quite grand like mine?"

He paused as if he couldn't bring himself to say it. "OK, it's Haandi."

I could stop myself giggling. "Handy? Like in the

121

word 'handyman'."

"You said you wouldn't laugh. Yes, it's like 'handyman' but is spelt differently. It's H-A-A-N-D-I."

"Haandi Wellington," I teased.

"No," said Kirsty. "'Wellington' was the name we choose when we came to Earth. Our name on Thaasia was..."

"Don't tell her, Mum," her son interrupted. "She'll only poke fun at me. Just call me 'Antony'."

"OK," I said, suppressing another giggle as he glared at me.

Kirsty stroked his arm and said: "I'm so sorry, Antony, but we had to change our names and identities. If it had become known who you and Annique really were then our enemies would have found us."

He refused to be placated. "You could have chosen a better name than 'Wellington'. And you might have given me some warning about all this, Mum. When we got to the field where the spaceship emerged I almost did a runner. It was so scary."

"You scared?" I ribbed. "It's a boys dream, isn't it - spaceships and all that stuff?"

"Only in films, Annique - not in real life, when you're not expecting it, and you suddenly learn you're an alien with another name. I was even more frightened when we landed here. I'd been looking forward to going to Disney World - not a completely different world. And I've just realised something - we'll never go to Disney World now, will we?"

"You dope," I chuckled.

Antony gave me a push. "Oh, yes, and you're so brave, aren't you? Anyway, when I stopped panicking, and had a look around, I found it was an incredible place. Dad showed me all the gadgets and inventions they have here - they're so amazing."

"Like those square boxes on the shelves in our rooms?"

"Yes, they're brilliant, but there is so much more," he assured me. "I got shown how to use lasers and ray guns, and now we might have to use them for real. It's mind-boggling. Just a few days ago we were sitting in our den reading books about adventures and now we're living one. It's so exciting, Annique, you must admit, it is."

"Exciting for you, but I'm worried sick about what is going to happen, and there's no sign of Waggles yet. We have to find him - I love him so much."

Stella made a scoffing sound and I turned abruptly to her.

"Stop being mean, Stella. You humanoids probably don't understand, but we humans get very attached to animals."

"Is that why you eat most of them?" she replied.

I didn't have an answer for that as I really enjoyed a good Sunday roast.

Lee came over to me. "I know how you feel," he said. "I'll go and ask if the craft carrying Waggles has landed."

With that, he hurried off.

While he was gone, I asked Graham how he'd arranged for the spaceship to come to Earth for us.

"We kept in constant touch with our friends on Thaasia, and they arranged for us to be transported when it became clear that Kaarn's men were close to finding out where we were."

Graham then explained that he'd never been an accountant, as I'd always believed, but a fully trained senior space travel officer.

"Just like Mr. Spock on the Enterprise?" Antony asked.

"Yes, I suppose so."

"That's really cool."

It all seemed incredible to me.

"Are there many other humanoids, like you and Graham, on Thaasia?" I asked Stella.

"There are, Annique, and unfortunately some of them support your Uncle Kaarn. Every important person is assigned a humanoid as a guardian, whose job is to protect them. Other humanoids serve as warriors."

"What are you exactly?" Antony asked.

"We are half human and half machine. As we explained to you previously, Graham and I were specially chosen to protect the King and Queen and were each given some of their genes so we became more like them."

"Part of the family," I suggested.

"Yes. It enabled us to become closer to Queen Lalia and King Daald and serve them better."

I leaned across and planted a kiss on Stella's cheek, feeling a sudden outpouring of love for her.

She said nothing but her smile was enough.

CHAPTER 34

Lee returned to inform us that Doctor Fraan, the head of security, had promised to meet with me the next morning.

"Surely he can tell us by now if the missing wasp has landed."

"Apparently there are some security issues," Lee said. "We will just have to be patient and wait until the morning."

*****

At 10am the following day we were ushered into the head of security's white-walled office where we were greeted by Doctor Fraan, a short yet imposing man whose hair had a strange green glow. He bowed to me and said: "It is a pleasure to meet you, Princess."

When we were all seated, he continued: "I believe you wanted to know about the missing mini-ship. I can now tell you that it crash-landed after being damaged by enemy fire. Fortunately, most of those on board escaped serious injury and finally managed to find their way here." But his expressionless face left me deeply worried.

"What about my dog Waggles? Is he safe?"

"I am very sorry to inform you that the dog is dead,"

he said solemnly.

The news I had been dreading had a devastating effect on me. The breath caught in my throat, causing me to choke. Antony came up to comfort me but it was some time before I could speak.

Dr Fraan continued. "Unfortunately, the dog was a plant."

"A plant? What on earth do you mean?"

"On Earth?" he queried, picking up on my figure of speech. "Yes, Kaarn's agents had finally discovered that you were on Earth and used the dog to spy on you by inserting a tracking device behind his ear."

"That's not possible," I gasped. "I was with Waggles the whole time. Isn't that right, Stella."

"Perhaps," she suggested, "the device was planted before you brought Waggles home."

"Impossible!" I snapped. "How could they know I would take the dog? A girl was stuffing Waggles into a sack and was about to throw him into a river when Antony and I rescued him."

The green-haired man again provided an explanation. "Kaarn and his men are very devious, Princess. Presumably the girl you saw was just pretending to throw the dog into the river. You were meant to see her do it and rescue him. The device inserted in the animal enabled Kaarn's agents to track all your movements. That is how they knew about your departure from Earth and were able to plan an attack on your spaceship."

"Good grief!" exclaimed Graham. "So they were lying in wait for us."

"Yes," Dr Fraan confirmed. "We did not know that Kaarn was planning to attack your ship.

Fortunately we were able to launch a counter attack and wipe out some of his fleet, we suffered casualties as well, but the most important thing was that you escaped."

Graham voiced more concern. "Does Kaarn know where we are now?"

Dr Fraan shook his head. "No," he said emphatically. This caused his green hair to stand up on end and emit a buzzing sound. "Fortunately, the medical team on your spacecraft removed the tracking device from the dog and it was deactivated. This was too late to prevent Kaarn's men pin-pointing your ship's position and launching their attack on it, but we believe they have been unable to find this secret location."

"Hopefully you are right," Lee replied. "But we can't be absolutely certain, can we?"

*****

Tears stung the back of my eyes as Stella walked me back to our room.

"It's so awful to know that Waggles is dead, Stella," I sobbed as the doors to my room swished open.

She responded by placing her hand on my shoulder and saying: "You must be strong, Annique."

But I did not take in her words. I was consumed with

grief and the most awful hatred for this monster Kaarn and his henchmen. They'd killed my parents and now Waggles.

Due to my evil uncle, I'd never known the love and protection my mother and father could have given me. Now he'd taken away my dear little friend Waggles.

Kaarn was a greedy, spoilt, nasty brute who thought nothing of destroying people's happiness to satisfy his own desires. How could two brothers be so different?

Stella spoke again, this time more firmly. "Thousands of your people have lost loved ones, but they will take heart when they learn that you have returned to Thaasia to claim the throne. You must be strong for them."

She was right. This was the moment I found my courage. I stopped longing for the past and became centred on the present, determined to fight along with all these brave people - *my* people.

I was their future queen and I must assume my role as their leader.

CHAPTER 35

Some time later Stella bought me a pink coloured drink in a tall glass. "This will help you sleep," she said, handing it to me as I lay on my bed.

"Thank you, Stella, but first I would like to know why my uncle is such an awful man. Why did he hate my mother and father enough to kill them?"

I placed the glass on the bedside table and Stella sighed as she pulled up a chair.

"Your father Daald was the first of three brothers - he was three years older than the middle son, Thaa, and almost six years older than Kaarn.

"Their mother Queen Zaalon was not blessed with good health and she died giving birth to Kaarn. But there was more tragedy to come."

"What happened?"

"Have patience, Annique, and I will tell you. Kaarn was a sickly child with a weak heart and he spent most of his time inside the castle. But one day his brothers took him fishing on a boat, unbeknown to their father King Paactus.

"Thaa saw a very large fish in the water and was so excited he jumped up and down, urging his brothers to catch it. This caused the boat to become unsteady, pitching all three of them over the side.

"Kaarn hit his head on one of the oars and was in difficulty. Daald managed to grab hold of Kaarn and drag him to the shore, but when Daald swam back there was no sign of Thaa. His dead body was discovered the next day. He had caught his foot in some reeds and drowned.

"The ordeal further weakened Kaarn's heart and he was seriously ill for a long time."

"But he must have recovered," I pointed out. "He's a monster now."

"Yes, he did eventually, though only after life-saving surgery. When he finally recovered people noticed Kaarn had changed drastically. He was no longer a loving son. Instead he became distant and cruel. His appearance also changed and he grew so much he ended up being the biggest man on the planet.

"King Paactus was already grief stricken following the deaths of his wife and Thaa. He literally died of a broken heart. It meant your father Daald had to take over the throne at the age of sixteen.

"Daald ruled Thaasia for seven years before marrying your mother Lalia. The alliance with her planet, Riola, caused great concern among many Thaasians because people on Riola had powers like you Annique. Kaarn was among those who feared these powers might be used against us."

"So what happened, Stella?" I asked, completely

engrossed in the horrific tale she was telling me.

"Things came to a head when your mother's most trusted and faithful aide, Prox, was stabbed to death by one of Kaarn's followers, a man called Raagar.

"Raagar was arrested and, under torture, claimed that he had been carrying out Kaarn's wishes. But your father Daald refused to believe that his brother had anything to do with it."

"Wasn't my father suspicious?"

"Kaarn swore his allegiance to the king, and Daald would not take any notice of allegations that his brother was plotting against him.

"It was a big mistake because Kaarn was able to get together a whole army of followers.

He must have realised after you were born that he would never be able to legitimately become our ruler. So at the banquet to officially confirm you as the next in line to the throne, on your second somara – birthday - Kaarn had your parents poisoned."

"What an evil man."

"Yes, Annique, he has become evil. But before that boating accident and him under going experimental surgery he had seemed quite normal. Then he changed dramatically, both physically and mentally."

Stella picked up the glass from the bedside table. "Now drink this down - it will help you relax and get some sleep."

"But how are we going to get rid of Kaarn?"

"No more now," she insisted. "Just relax."

Taking hold of my little locket, which I still wore around my neck along with the pendant Antony had given me, I looked at the photos of Daald and Lalia, my parents, who I had originally believed were my grandparents. I studied their faces more carefully than before. Although I had my mother's long, black hair and purple eyes, my skin was much paler, like my father's.

I wished with every beat of my heart that I'd known them. All I had now was a little photograph which I treasured - and a burning desire to make Kaarn pay for killing them.

CHAPTER 36

After Stella had brought me breakfast the next morning, Graham asked me to go with him to the science laboratory.

As we walked along a wide corridor, I glanced at his neck to make certain that there were no longer any wires hanging out of him.

I hadn't seen much of Graham since arriving on Thaasia. Maybe he preferred to keep his distance now I was acknowledged as a member of the royal family. It made me sad because I still thought of him as my father, but I realised he had been given the task of protecting me on Earth and delivering me to Thaasia in one piece. Perhaps to him it was simply a case of task accomplished!

Stella, however, seemed different. She still fussed over me, making sure that I had enough to eat and looked smart. That old mantra 'a clean ship is a happy ship' was still her maxim. But she was also trying to prepare me for a lot of new and strange things on this planet where she and Graham had lived for many years before having to flee.

When we reached the science lab, Graham introduced me to the Head of Technology, Raavalla. She was a tall, strange looking but nevertheless attractive woman, with blue hair that was in different lengths. It was longer on the right side where a streak of silver ran through the blue. Her skin was so pale it looked bloodless, and her lips were thin, as though drawn by a pencil.

She showed me around her lab with a passion which I thought bordered on the manic.

My attention focused on a line of large glass jars filled with gruesome body parts and organs.

"Those are our SPs," Raavalla informed me.

"SPs?"

"Spare parts taken from citizens when they die."

I was about to express my shock, but Raavalla's deep brown eyes seemed to bore right through me, causing me to remain silent.

As she continued to show me around, it was obvious that she was deeply passionate about her work.

We passed another row of jars which contained smaller parts. "Some of these look as if they're from children," I said.

This prompted her to explain. "A few years ago a new law was decreed that families on Thaasia who do not serve in the king's army can only have two children. If it is found they have disobeyed that ruling then the third child is taken away as soon as it is discovered."

"Taken away to where?"

She broke off eye contact and glanced at the jars.

My mouth dropped open with shock. "That's terrible. Why was this allowed to happen?"

"Our King Kaarn thought this would prevent more

people joining the rebels. I used to work for him and brought some of the SPs here with me when I defected."

I detected approval in her tone as she continued: "The body parts can be developed or used for experiments."

"I'm sorry, I have to leave. I can't listen to any more." I turned away, but what Raavalla said next caused me to stop abruptly.

"Before you go it may interest you to learn what happened to your dog."

"I already know he was killed after the attack on our spaceship. Are you telling me you have his body in one of your jars?"

"Let me explain. There were actually two devices in the dog's body. The second was in his neck and enabled Kaarn's men to hear what was being said by anyone in close proximity to him. The medical team on the spaceship did not have time to remove it so they brought the dog to me and I operated on him."

I glared at her. "Does that mean he died during the operation? Why wasn't I told? I would not have given you permission to operate."

"I am sorry, Princess, but the priority was to retrieve the device, and at the same time help develop surgery that can save lives..."

Her words did not register. I felt devastated and was about to fall into a deep black pit of emotion as my brain became bombarded with images of my little friend Waggles.

Raavalla's cold, unsympathetic voice suddenly

penetrated my numbness. "...although the dog was technically dead, we inserted crannos into it as an experiment, and are waiting to see if this restores his heart and brain functions. Crannos are like the nanobots your Earthling friends have developed. Ours are much more advanced since we used them on Kaarn years ago."

Gulping with shock and new hope, I blurted out: "Are you telling me that my dog may come back to life?"

"It's a possibility, yes, but only for observation purposes. The dog is very important to us because there are no similar animals on Thaasia for us to experiment on. If it works then we will open him up to see how the crannos have connected with his heart and brain tissue."

All the anger I had been bottling up since our spaceship was attacked suddenly exploded.

My fists bunched as they had when confronting the school bullies and I struggled to control the purple mist which suddenly appeared in my eyes.

"If you are asking me if you can experiment on my dog, the answer is 'no', never. If you touch one hair on his head without my permission I will not be answerable for the consequences."

"I don't think I *asked* you," she said in a sarcastic tone as she walked towards the exit door, pulling it open quickly and standing aside to let me out.

My head buzzed as I tried without success to control my powers. Suddenly an explosion of purple lifted Raavalla off her feet into the air.

"Put me down at once," she yelled as she floated above my head.

"Don't mess with me," I shouted back. "I want you to restore my dog to life and not experiment on him any further. I hope I make myself clear."

"You do, you do. Now let me down."

Graham, who had been at the other end of the laboratory, came rushing up. "Put her down, Annique," he yelled.

This firm instruction brought me back to my senses. I closed my eyes briefly and heard her crash to the floor.

She rose to her feet, rubbing her elbow, but otherwise apparently unhurt. Her angry expression changed into a forced smile. "Keeping the dog alive long term is not my decision to make," she said. "Commander Geddaall would have to give his consent."

"Then I will get his consent," I said. And, with that, I stormed out of her laboratory, followed by Graham.

As I strode down the corridor, he called out to me.

"Hold on, Annique. I don't think you have thought this out."

"What do you mean?" I challenged, turning abruptly.

"You adopted the dog against Stella's advice. As a result of you bringing it with us Kaarn's men were able to track down and destroy our spaceship, killing several of the crew as well as some of those who tried to rescue us. And the second device found in the dog may have put everyone here at risk. In the circumstances Commander Geddaall may not be willing to grant a request to have Waggles handed back to you."

His words hit home and I was consumed with guilt.

"I'm so sorry if I put people in danger, but it was Kaarn who was to blame for their deaths.

The point is Waggles is my dog and I love him."

Graham now spoke in a kinder tone, but his words sent a shiver through my whole body. "So maybe it was not a good idea to antagonise Raavalla - the one person who is capable of bringing your dog back from the dead."

CHAPTER 37

I couldn't think what was the best thing for me to do so I went to see Antony in his room and told him the whole story about what had happened to Waggles.

"You will need to ask Commander Geddaall to let Waggles be handed over to you," he advised.

"But what if he refuses?"

"It would be difficult for him to go against the wishes of a Princess," he said, with a huge grin on his face. "Why don't you talk to Raavalla first and find out if she can bring Waggles back to life."

"The problem is I can't stand her, Antony, and I can tell that she doesn't like me."

"Perhaps you should start by apologising for what you did to her. It's important you get Raavalla on your side. I'll come with you to the lab."

"I've just told you I hate her - why don't you listen?"

"OK, OK, prickly pants, but it's what you need to do."

We went straight to the laboratory but the door was locked and nobody answered when we knocked. I started to panic until Antony managed to calm me down. "Don't worry," he said soothingly. "We'll come back first thing in the morning. Raavalla is unlikely to do anything to

Waggles overnight."

"But what if she does? You don't know everything old boot face." It gave me some satisfaction to throw an insult back at him after his crack about 'prickly pants'.

Ignoring my outburst, Antony popped some gum in his mouth.

"Where did you get that from?"

"I stuffed some in my socks. I won't tell you where I put the rest. Now correct me if you think I'm wrong as usual, but first Raavalla has got to bring Waggles back to life - and that's what you want, isn't it?"

*****

Our early morning visit to the lab was a frustrating waste of time. There was no sign of Raavalla and her assistant told us we would have to return later because she was sleeping after working until late into the night.

When I returned alone two hours later I almost bumped into Raavalla coming out of the lab and walking purposefully towards me.

"I assume you know the whereabouts of your dog," she said bluntly, staring into my eyes and ignoring the usual head bowing protocol that I'd got used to receiving since I arrived on Thaasia.

"He needs more time to recover following the operation I performed on him last night."

I glared at her. "I told you not to touch my dog without my permission. Are you saying you operated on him anyway and that he has now disappeared?"

"I think you know very well that he has."

"Can you please tell me what you are talking about, Raavalla? I have no idea where Waggles is."

"I checked last night to see if the crannos I had injected into your dog had fully restored his heart and brain functions. The surgery was so successful that after a few hours he regained consciousness. I personally kept him under observation during the night, but when I returned this morning he had gone."

"How could he have suddenly disappeared?"

"I thought you had taken him."

"Of course I didn't. You don't think Kaarn's men have got him?"

"I doubt that," she said with a rather strange expression on her face.

'What was she hiding?' I wondered.

"Poor Waggles. Where can he be? We must search for him. Perhaps he simply escaped from your laboratory. He might even have gone looking for me." I started walking briskly back along the corridor and she followed me.

"There's something you need to know first," Raavalla blurted out, running to catch up with me. "He's...changed."

"Changed. What do you mean changed? What have you done to my dog?"

I noticed she avoided making eye contact as she continued. "He has grown and become much stronger. When he woke up I had to restrain him. He's a very powerful dog now. He may hurt people so I would ask you most fervently to return him to me if you find him. I need to continue my tests and make him less aggressive. I promise that he will not feel any pain."

"Don't you dare do any more experiments on my dog," I said as we continued walking.

When we approached my room I could see Stella waiting outside for me, looking very anxious.

"A large animal tried to get in here," she said. "It was yelping and scrapping your door.

When I came to see what was going on it ran off. I have never seen such a strange creature – it looked like a dog but was almost as big as a lion."

CHAPTER 38

Antony and I went back into the corridor. "Waggles, Waggles," I called frantically, looking left and right, but there was no sign of him.

"What shall we do now?" asked Antony. "Perhaps we had better split up."

"Yes. You go and search for him - I'll return to my room and wait with Stella. He's already been there once and he may come back."

The time ticked by slowly. Whenever I heard a noise outside the door I went to investigate, but Waggles wasn't there.

"Sit down and rest, Annique," Stella told me. "I have been in touch with Graham on my communicator and he is looking for the dog, too. We just have to wait for news."

Antony returned to check if I was alright. "My Dad is also looking," he said. Don't worry - we'll find him."

"I'm going to search myself," I told them, but just as I approached the door I heard a very loud woof coming from the other side.

"Waggles," I called out excitedly, wrenching the door open, expecting my little pup to jump into my arms. But I was so shocked by what I saw I had to gasp for breath.

A monster-sized animal with a big sloppy smile on his face jumped on top of me, knocking me off my feet.

"Get off you ugly creature," cried Stella as she and Antony tried to pull him back, but even their combined strength was no match for this huge beast.

I could not make any protests as I was being covered with long, sloppy wet licks. If this was Waggles, he looked completely different. Gone was the cute little dog with the cute floppy ears. In his place was a large, muscular animal with big eyes, massive paws and a gigantic mouth filled with strong white teeth, who swished his tail wildly in excitement.

"Waggl..." I tried to catch my breath between licks. "Waggles stop." But the licks continued.

"Sit...SIT!" I commanded. Finally he stopped and, after a moment's hesitation, sat with his long wet tongue dangling out of one side of his mouth.

"DOWN!" I said firmly, pointing to the floor.

This time he immediately dropped to the floor, resting his head on his large paws, but not taking his eyes off me for a second.

"*Waggles,*" I said softly. "Waggles, is it really you?"

He cocked his head to one side and whined.

"Oh, Waggles," I cried, throwing myself onto his large body and rubbing my fingers through his black silky fur. One ear stuck up and he lapsed into the happy, silly grin I loved so much. We rolled on the floor, me laughing and then crying with relief, him barking and turning over so that I could tickle his tummy, before he nearly crushed me in his excitement.

"We must be quiet or they'll come and take him away," urged Antony.

Waggles suddenly stood in front of me, growling as though he had understood what Antony had said.

"You're right, Antony," I replied. "We must hide him from Raavalla. I don't want her do any more experiments on him. Waggles may look a bit like a monster now, but he's the same friendly dog he used to be."

I tried to push Waggles under the bed, but he simply lifted the back end of it off the floor.

Stella took charge of the situation by reminding me: "You are Raavalla's superior, Annique.

She cannot go against your wishes."

I wasn't convinced after my previous clashes with the Head of Technology.

Suddenly there was an enormous explosion, followed by another, which caused the foundations to shake.

"Whatever is it?" I cried out.

The door was suddenly thrust open and there was dependable old Graham. "Follow me," he instructed. "We are under attack again."

Lee and Kirsty appeared and we all raced along the corridor, with Waggles bounding along next to me. Graham led us down some stairs on to another floor.

I could hear others also running down the stairs. When I turned to look I saw Doctor Fraan and a tall grey-haired, bearded man holding the hand of a small child.

Doctor Fraan overtook us when we reached a short corridor. He unlocked a door at the end of it and called "This way."

We entered a reinforced chamber which had computer screens on every wall. We all settled down as best we could in the confined space and waited, relieved to have found somewhere safe.

"What's going on?" I asked anxiously.

My question was answered immediately when Commander Geddaall appeared on the screens.

"This is your commander speaking," his voice boomed. "Please do not panic. Kaarn's men have been launching a series of missiles and two of them exploded almost immediately above us.

But they now seem to be aiming further afield which suggests they do not know our exact location and are bombing the whole area.

"There have been a few casualties, but hopefully the danger has passed."

When the picture of the commander faded, Antony asked: "What do we do now?"

"We wait," said Doctor Fraan, raising his voice emphatically. This prompted his green hair to shoot up in the air and buzz while he continued speaking. "If there are no more explosions in the next fifteen minutes I think we can assume the threat to us is over. The Commander will decide if we should launch any counter-attacks."

The little boy was now sitting between me and the bearded man, fear etched across his face. "What's your name?" I asked gently.

The man answered for him. "His name is Saam. He's my son."

"Hello Saam, my name is Annique." He didn't look at me or reply so I tried another tactic.

"This is my dog Waggles." I began to stroke Waggles' head and he responded by rolling his eyes, reminding me of Scooby-Doo. The little boy giggled, and it lifted the tension.

"A few weeks ago Waggles was very small, but he's grown so much that he's as big as a lion now, isn't he? 'Waggles' no longer sounds the right name for him. Can you help me think of another one please?"

Saam bit his bottom lip, snuggled closer to the man, and frowned.

It seemed he would not answer, but suddenly he replied: "*Captain* Waggles."

Antony laughed as my dog cocked his head and wagged his tail.

"Captain Waggles is a splendid name and he seems to like it," I said. "I bet you know what we're saying, Captain Waggles, you clever boy." I stroked him and encouraged Saam to do the same.

Stella sighed loudly.

"I'm Jamas," said the man. "And you must be Princess Annaaqualalia. I'm the brother of your mother, Queen Lalia, and came here from our planet Riola to help the resistance movement fight Kaarn following the death of my beloved sister and her husband King Daald."

"Wow! So you're my Uncle."

"Yes, but you can call me Jamas if you like. Tell me, Annique, how did you come by such a large dog?"

"He was only a puppy when I found him on Earth," I explained. "He got hurt on the spaceship that brought us here...well actually he died."

Jamas seemed puzzled, as he was clearly looking at a very much alive Captain Waggles.

"I mean he *was* dead, but Raavalla used crannos to bring him back to life, and now he's huge."

"Not again!" Jamas snapped. "Surely they've learnt their lesson by now."

He put his left hand over his forehead and drew his large fingers down his face, looking exasperated. "Crannos may be able to save life, but they can also do great harm," he said. "Years ago they used them on Kaarn in a similar operation. It would have been better if he'd died."

"You mean because he's so wicked?"

"He wasn't wicked before they operated - only afterwards," Jamas revealed. "Kaarn was seriously ill after a boating accident that killed his brother Thaa."

"Yes, Stella told me about how he was almost drowned like Thaa."

Jamas paused before continuing. "Kaarn had a weak heart and almost died, too. He was in a coma for days. The scientists on Thaasia had been experimenting with crannos and, although the technology was not as advanced as it is today, they felt justified in injecting Kaarn with them.

"They probably saved his life, but he was no longer the same when he recovered. Before the operation he had been a normal boy in both shape and character but the crannos turned him into an over-sized monster, like your dog."

"My dog's not a monster," I insisted.

"Maybe not - but Kaarn most certainly is."

CHAPTER 39

A loud knock at the door interrupted our conversation and Doctor Fraan went to answer it.

Captain Waggles pushed his huge body in front of me and growled softly as if he expected trouble. Saam tried to hide behind us. "It's okay," I murmured. "No one will harm you, Saam."

I was more confident now that I had Captain Waggles to protect me.

A familiar head poked round the door - it was Raavalla, the woman I had come to hate.

"The attack's over," she said. Then, after going into a huddle with Doctor Fraan and exchanging whispered comments, she turned to address us again. "You should all come with me. I will take you back to your rooms."

As we exited the chamber and climbed the stairs, I wondered how many more times I would have to run and hide. We'd been lucky so far. The smell of scorched flesh was awful as injured soldiers were being helped along the corridor towards the medical centre.

This was further evidence of the maniac my Uncle Kaarn had become. Would the crannos that had changed him so much eventually have a similar effect on my dear

Captain Waggles?

I was distracted by Saam who took hold of my hand.

"You are a brave boy, aren't you?" I said.

"Yes I am. And I'm only five years old," he confided.
Jamas and I burst out laughing.

*****

"What happens now?" I asked Stella when we got
back to my room.

She turned and handed me a note. "Keep this safe,
Annique. If we get separated or are in any danger you will
need to know who you can trust and how to contact them.
Are you wearing your bracelet?"

"Yes, I never take it off."

"Good. The five people on that list have similar
bracelets. Doctor Fraan has named them 'The Band Of
Five' and he feels they are best able to help you. Just say
the number you want and give your code name, which is
Purple Mist."

I settled down on the bed, with Captain Waggles at my
feet, and read the contact numbers for The Band Of Five:

101 – Jamas

102 – Lee

103 – Graham

104 – Stella

105 – Raavalla

Two of the names surprised me. Jamas I had only just
met and knew very little about him, while Raavalla was

someone I would never trust.

CHAPTER 40

"It's become too dangerous for you to stay here," Stella told me the following morning. "We must leave."

"I don't feel anywhere is safe on this planet, Stella. But I thought the attacks on us had stopped."

"They have. The problem is Kaarn's men could return because he will be searching everywhere for you. In the circumstances Commander Geddaall thinks it is now time to launch a major counter attack, but to first take you to a new location."

"Where are we going this time?"

"Somewhere Kaarn will never expect you to be - a secret cave beneath his castle."

Seeing my look of horror, Stella added: "Don't worry, the Band of Five will be there to protect you."

"Does that mean Raavalla will be coming with us?" I asked, unable to mask my disapproval.

"Yes. She has been assigned to safeguard you, together with Jamas, Lee, Graham and myself," Stella reminded me. "The Commander would not have given her such a responsibility if he was not confident that she could be relied upon."

*****

Saam and Captain Waggles joined us in boarding a hybrid flying ship which had specially-fitted air-cushions to enable it to also travel over land, water or ice like a hovercraft.

Covered in cloaking devices to make our craft invisible when airborne, we headed towards Kaarn's castle in the city of Shaalt.

Captain Waggles, who needed a seat to himself as he was too big to sit on my lap now, spent much of the trip growling at Raavalla until I finally managed to make him shut up by giving him a biscuit.

Looking out of the small window, as we approached the outskirts of the city, I saw a mass of rocks beyond which was a silver lake and blue ice glaciers. We landed not far from the lake, cloaked in a white mist.

When the doors swished open I got a shock at the change of temperature. It was freezing.

Stella had made me wear a thick jacket for the journey but this was colder than anything I had ever experienced on Earth and my teeth started to chatter.

"Don't worry - we've brought some warm sleeping bags," Graham assured me, handing each of us one of them, wrapped in a pack to be strapped to our backs.

We all left the craft, with Graham and Raavalla leading the way, closely followed by Jamas, Saam, Antony and his parents as we walked past a cluster of huge rocks. Soon we came to a clump of tall trees and bushes of many different colours.

This planet was beautiful in places but I still missed the countryside on Earth.

Did they have seasons here? Spring and Autumn were my favourites back home. Yes, I still thought of Earth as my home.

It was early evening, and Graham told us we would have to wait until night fall before getting back into our little multi-purpose craft to glide over the lake to the cave under the cover of darkness. We had brought food, sleeping bags and insulated tents which were speedily erected under the cover of large rocks and bushes.

"Why are we out here getting freezing cold?" I asked nobody in particular as I hugged myself in an unsuccessful attempt to get warm. "Surely we could have stayed in our wasp."

Graham provided the answer. "Although the craft's cloaking device makes it invisible in the air, if we had flown any closer to the castle Kaarn could still have picked us up on his radar. I'm hoping that our craft will not be noticed where we have left it on the other side of the rocks but there is the risk that Kaarn's men could spot it. If they did and we had remained on board we would be sitting chickens."

"I think you mean sitting ducks," I corrected.

We sat down and Stella handed out the food.

After eating, I stood up to peer through the trees at the lake. The mist was lifting slightly and I could see a mountain covered with glowing silver minerals to the right, while to the left, in the far distance, was a huge, imposing white building, surrounded by a glittering red wall.

"What an amazing sight!" said Antony, coming to stand beside me. "The royal residence is really something, isn't it?"

"Yes. When Graham and Stella told me of my parents' deaths in the big hall, I had imagined a castle like the ones on Earth, centuries old with turrets, a drawbridge and surrounded by a moat.

This looks more like something from a science fiction film, though the domes are a bit like those in Russia. But I can't see a single window."

"I bet it's nice and warm in there - I'm freezing," Antony replied. "I'm going to get into my sleeping bag."

"OK, I'll just spend a few more minutes here," I told him, still looking at the castle while stroking Captain Waggles' large head.

"Magnificent, isn't it?" said my Uncle Jamas, joining me as Antony hurried off. "The castle is only spoilt by being adorned with orange and green flags - the colours of that awful man Kaarn."

"Yes, it's lovely, but not at all what I expected to see," I explained. "Why aren't there any windows?"

"That's an illusion. From the inside you would see many windows, but they all have special protective shields. Your mother requested many changes to ensure the castle was safer after the adverse reaction by some people to her marriage to King Daald. They resented Daald marrying someone from another planet who had special powers."

"You must have been very close to her."

"Yes, I was," Jamas reflected sadly. "My sister was such a wonderful person. Those who met Lalia were captivated by her beauty. And her smile would melt your heart. Your father told me he'd fallen in love with her from the moment he saw her.

"She was also so kind and gentle - apart from those occasions when she used her powers to conjure up a purple mist to protect herself or others. I once saw her surround Kaarn with the mist, pinning him to a wall until he promised to stop hitting a servant after some petty squabble. She was an amazing woman, but I think that Kaarn turned against her from that moment. He never forgave her for humiliating him.

"I had returned to Riola shortly after you were born and I was shattered to hear that my beloved Lalia and Daald had been poisoned. I came back to Thaasia to join the rebel army and help to topple the man who had killed them."

"I can make a purple mist appear, too," I told Jamas without thinking. I hoped Stella and Graham would not be cross with me for revealing my secret, but then I realised he must have this special power as well because he came from Riola like my mother.

Jamas studied me closely before saying: "You look like your mother. You have Lalia's lovely silky dark hair and warm eyes. You were so very young when your parents were killed, but they loved you very much."

"Did you get to know my father well?"

"Quite well. Daald was kept busy with affairs of state but he found time to teach me how to ride a Zaak"

"What's a Zaak?"

"It's a large animal and can run very fast. I suppose it looks similar to one of your camels on Earth - but without the humps."

We stood together for a few minutes in silence, looking over the lake. It was incredible that a few weeks ago I would probably have been sitting in our den, waiting for Antony to come in chewing his gum. I wondered if they had horses here, as I could imagine riding with Antony. It made me think of Bella and Crispin. who I would probably never see again.

"Well," said Jamas. "I must go to check if Saam is sleeping soundly in our tent."

"I expect he's been missing his mother," I muttered, uttering my thoughts aloud.

"Presumably you didn't bring her with you to Thaasia."

"Samm is not actually my son by birth. I adopted him because he was the third child of a Thaasian couple who refused to serve in Kaarn's army and therefore he would have been put to death under the king's crazy ruling."

"How could Kaarn impose such a terrible law?" I asked.

"He wanted to deter anyone who did not show their

loyalty to him. He feared that those with big families would be better equipped to rise against him. The people of Thaasia will be so grateful when this madman is toppled and you take over as queen.

*****

"Wake up, Annique, wake up." Stella's voice, close to my ear, caused me to come out of a deep, but troubled sleep, in which I'd dreamed of fighting all manner of unrecognisable beasts with huge heads.

"OK," I answered, still huddled in my sleeping bag. I rubbed my eyes and struggled to see through the darkness. My feet were numb with the cold.

Captain Waggles yawned and stretched as I patted him with one of my gloved hands.

Getting out of the sleeping bag, I began shivering and realised it had become even colder, with the the sun having disappeared to be replaced by a large purple moon.

When we had packed the sleeping bags and tents away, I noticed that the moon had turned the blue ice caps along the lake into the same purple colour. It was eerie but beautiful.

I must have looked really scared because Jamas came over and took my hand in his.

"Don't worry little one, we will look after you," he said tenderly. "Soon you will become the Queen of Thaasia and will move into the castle with your own staff."

"I know Stella and Graham are humanoids, Uncle

Jamas, but I feel they are my parents now and want them to stay with me always."

"Yes, they have looked after you well. It has become their life's work to protect you. And if the Queen of Thaasia wants them to stay with her, then no one will go against her wishes."

"I'm so glad you're my uncle," I told him, with my eyes misting over. He smiled and I learned over to gently kiss him on the check.

I then glanced across the lake at the castle, on which the moon was casting a purple beam of light.

Suddenly a terrifying thought struck me - we'll soon be going into the lion's den. My fears returned.

CHAPTER 41

As we moved towards our craft, I asked Jamas how we would get into the cave.

"Our ship will take us over the lake and then right up to the cave entrance," he said. "We could not risk going in daylight because Kaarn's guards would almost certainly have detected us."

Like me, Antony seemed concerned. "Is the cave really safe?" he asked.

Jamas smiled. "It really is the last place Kaarn would think to look for us. So we should be safe while our army attacks his castle. There is not just one underground tunnel but several of them.

Local people don't go in the caves because of stories about them being haunted." He chuckled as he spoke and winked at me.

"Was it you who spread the rumours, Uncle Jamas?"

He laughed again.

"Actually, there are some creatures in the caves so we must be careful."

We all climbed aboard our craft and were soon skimming across the lake. Raavalla and I exchanged glares, but I was comforted by Antony squeezing my hand. Saam was obviously enjoying the ride as was Captain Waggles, who wagged his tale and ears in turn!

Within minutes we'd arrived. We left the craft in deep undergrowth, and Graham led the way through the darkness.

Kirsty slipped on the muddy surface, knocking into Raavalla, who, in turn, bumped into Captain Waggles. He snarled at her and then started barking.

Graham turned round, clearly annoyed. "Annique, you must keep him quiet, or we'll be discovered."

When we got to the cave Captain Waggles let himself down again by bounding into the icy entrance and promptly sliding on to his backside, which resulted in more barking!

"You should never have brought the dog," Raavalla snarled in my ear.

"You're wrong," I replied coldly. "Waggles is the best form of protection I could have."

We trudged along, trying to keep our footing in the dark. Eventually Stella announced:

"We're far enough inside the cave now and out of sight of the castle so I'll switch on my lights."

Before I could ask her what she meant the red rims around her eyes lit up like torch beams, as did Graham's a few seconds later. The cave was floodlit. "Wow," Antony shouted, that's amazing."

I was speechless. No words could describe how I felt about seeing Stella and Graham like this. They both looked so alien, so robotic. I clasped my hands together tightly, trying to hide the fact that they were shaking. These were the two people I'd always thought of as my parents.

Seeing them like this unnerved me.

We walked further and further into the cold dankness of the cave, with Stella and Graham lighting the way and Jamas carrying little Saam on his shoulders.

"Shhh...did you hear that?" Graham stopped suddenly, holding out his hand for us to remain still.

"Maybe it's a Gerzil," said Kirsty.

"Do they really exist?" Antony said. "You used to tell me stories about them when I was little - I thought you made them up."

"They are real," his dad assured him. "There used to be lots of them in these caves so we must be careful."

"What are Gerzil's, Antony?" I whispered in his ear.

"Big jelly-like creatures that live in the caves. Mum used to sing me this song:

"The Gerzil is watching, take care or he'll come,

He sees all the bad things you do, every one.

Don't try to hide from his big yellow eyes,

They will see right through any disguise"

I turned to Jamas. "Did you see any Gerzils when you were staying in the castle, Uncle?"

"No, Annique, but I could hear them chanting to each other at night."

Suddenly the communication bracelet on his wrist buzzed and he answered it.

"Hello...yes...okay we'll wait a while then."

"That was the Commander. He has advised us not to go any further because his troops are preparing to attack the castle. So let's find ourselves a comfy rock to sit on." He laughed at his own joke as we all looked around for somewhere to sit.

"Why don't you get some sleep, Annique?" Lee suggested. "You, too, Antony."

"But what about the Gerzils?" I persisted.

"Don't worry," Jamas assured me. "We will keep a look out and we have our lasers. Now may I recommend that we all sit and wait for instructions. Has anyone got any food left, I'm starving?"

Stella opened a rucksack she'd been carrying with her, taking out a flask and a paper bag.

"Here, drink some water and eat these."

They were small little biscuits that tasted like cheese and there were enough to share with the others, although Raavalla was fiddling with her bracelet and did not seem interested in eating.

Stella, you should have some, too," I said.

"Graham and I don't need to eat every day, Annique. Don't you remember when we were living on Earth how little Graham and I ate?"

"I thought you were always on a diet, but you did like baking lots of cakes and pies."

"I did, but you and Antony ate most of them."

The biscuits were very filling, but hunger wasn't the only bodily function I needed to satisfy.

I was bursting and was quite sure Captain Waggles needed to pee, too.

"Stella," I whispered. "Where can I relieve myself?"

"Well, go behind some rocks, Annique."

"I'll come, too, I need to go as well," said Antony.

"But not with us," I told him curtly. He nodded and moved in the opposite direction, urging Captain Waggles to follow him.

"Don't you dare - he's staying with me."

"Scaredy-cat," Antony called back before disappearing into the dark.

A few minutes later, while making our way back to the others, I felt a sudden chill, and heard a noise above me.

Looking up, I saw two enormous large yellow eyes peering at us.

I screamed as a huge creature whooshed down from the ceiling on to Antony, Captain Waggles and me. It was like a gigantic blob of jelly. We were pinned to the floor, struggling for breath as hot, sticky, yellow fluid came out of the creature's mouth. It covered my head - and smelled like sick.

Scratching and clawing to escape, I bit into my disgusting attacker. All I could hear were muffled shouts and barking as Antony and Captain Waggles tried to fight it off, too.

In the frenzy I conjured up a blinding purple mist,

which engulfed the monster, causing it to crystallise as it crashed violently into the cave wall. It exploded into a thousand pieces.

One of the creature's eyes rolled round the floor like a giant yellow marble. I was shaking with shock after just killing this horrible monster, but tried to wipe the foul, putrid grunge from my eyes.

The others ran up to us. "Annique, Antony, are you alright?" shouted Kirsty.

"I just can't get this awful stuff off me," I gasped, spitting some of the sticky fluid from my mouth.

"Hold your head down," Stella commanded as she poured some water over me.

I retched. Stella remained calm, however, and wiped the grunge away. Blinking repeatedly, I was eventually able to see. Antony and Captain Waggles, like me, were covered in slime and my enormous dog was running around in circles, chasing his now yellow tail.

I turned to Antony, who had just finished wiping his face. "Was that a Gerzil?"

He didn't reply. Instead he held his breath for a moment and then violently sneezed. A long slimy rope of snot hung from his nose, causing me to vomit again.

"Ugh... that's disgusting, Antony."

"Sorry," he stammered. But before he could remove it, Captain Waggles pounced on top of him and started licking it as the pair of them rolled around the floor.

"Oh, that's gross!" I shouted, but I suddenly got the

giggles. Some of the others began laughing, too - but not Stella, Graham or Raavalla.

CHAPTER 42

We had been waiting a few hours when Jamas' bracelet received a message.

"Lock onto these co-ordinates and dial the number 6987," he told us.

We did so on our bracelets and could see the grave face of the Commander. "Are you alright - is the Princess safe?" he asked.

"Yes," replied Jamas. "Annique is with us in the main cave and we are all OK. What about you?"

"Our initial attack on the castle did not have the surprise effect we were planning," the Commander revealed. "Many of Kaarn's spacecraft engaged us in battle - it was almost as if someone had warned him we were coming. But we acquitted ourselves reasonably well. The battle is still going on in the air and we have not yet entered the castle. I will contact you again when it is safe for you to move."

"Thank you, Commander."

The picture disappeared from the screens on our bracelets and the connection was cut.

"So we must sit here and wait until our troops gain control," said Graham.

"But there is no guarantee that they will," Kirsty pointed out. "You heard what the Commander said - Kaarn's men were prepared for the attack. Someone must have alerted them."

"We can still win, can't we Dad?" Antony asked Lee who had been discussing the situation with Jamas.

"I hope so, son. If we can win the battle in the air our soldiers will storm the castle. They are all willing to risk their lives rather than continue living under Kaarn's rule. We must keep believing that we will beat him."

Captain Waggles yelped and stuck out his large tongue.

"Can I give him some water, Stella?" I asked.

"Sorry Annique, but it's all gone. I used the last of it washing that muck off your face."

Raavalla delved into her knapsack and took out a bottle which she offered me. "You can all have some of this. It's best you all drink first before offering it to the dog."

Taking it from her, I uttered a 'thank you' and took a swig myself, then handed the bottle to the others. They drank it in turn except Saam who was asleep. Waggles finally got to slurp what was left.

Feeling suddenly sleepy and swaying slightly, I leaned back against the rough cave wall behind me, struggling to keep my eyes open.

"Stella…I don't...feel well. I…" my words began to slur as I slipped down slowly onto the floor and passed out.

CHAPTER 43

My head was throbbing when I regained consciousness. I was sitting against a rock, with a blindfold over my eyes, and not able to move my arms as my hands were tied together behind my back.

"So our *Princess* is awake at last." It was Raavalla's voice. "I wondered how long it would take you to wake up. It's been over an hour since I gave you the drug in the water that knocked you and your friends out."

I struggled in vain to loosen my bindings, realising it was impossible to touch my bracelet to warn anyone.

The blindfold was not fully covering my left eye and I could just make out two other Thaasians, a man and a woman both in uniforms, who were standing on what looked like large skateboards without wheels. One was holding the side of his head, with blood trickling through his fingers.

"Let me introduce you to my colleagues Mikkel and Yanni. I summoned them from the castle to help me and they've just arrived by our new updated transporter. Unfortunately we're encountering a few snags in breaking down body particles on departure and rebuilding them on arrival. Poor Mikkel has arrived minus an ear. But I digress.

We'll soon be taking you to King Kaarn."

I was stunned as I squinted through my blindfold at the one-eared Mikkel, but I recovered to rage at Raavalla: "So you're the traitor who tipped off Kaarn's men that the Commander was launching an attack."

"Yes, I warned them. But I'm no traitor. I stayed true to my beliefs. I've always been loyal to Kaarn."

"What have you done with my friends and my dog?" I demanded, trying to turn round but only succeeding in almost toppling over.

Raavalla laughed. "They are laying on the ground behind you. They came round before you so we put them back to sleep with our stun guns. The female humanoid put up quite a fight. Yaani blew one of her arms clean off before deactivating her."

"Please don't tell me Stella's dead," I sobbed. "I couldn't bare it."

"Don't pretend you have feelings for that piece of metal," scoffed 'The Mad Scientist'. "She has no feelings for you. She's not programmed to love - protect yes; love, no. I suppose she could be repaired but it's more likely Kaarn will want her and your other friends to be destroyed."

Anger boiled inside me and purple zigzag daggers of light lit up behind my mask, making my headache worse. If only I could focus properly.

"Stella is irreplaceable, Raavalla. I will always think of her as my mother. Why have you done this - I thought you were on our side?"

"I'm on the side of the people of Thaasia. You are weak - you'll never be equal to a Thaasian woman. We are strong. You have been on Earth too long. I could never follow you."

The slight gap in the blindfold enabled me to look closer at her two colleagues. I had never seen the bearded man before, but the red-haired female seemed vaguely familiar. She was quite young, maybe around 17 or 18. Her hair was thick and curly. It was the hair more than anything else that I found familiar. Where had I seen her before? My thoughts were interrupted by a movement behind me, followed by a growl. It was Captain Waggles - he had regained consciousness.

"It's the wretched dog," snapped Mikkel. "I thought you had used your stun gun on him, Yaani."

"I did, but the animal is so big and powerful he has come round much quicker than normal."

Captain Waggles was snarling at Yaani as he edged towards her.

"Perhaps I should silence him for good with..."

"No," Raavalla interrupted. "I want to conduct some more experiments on him when all this is over. I think a double stun should do the trick."

As she spoke she obviously used her stun gun. Two blasts rang out and Waggles collapsed in a heap on the floor next to me.

"Oh, my poor Waggles," I gasped, only able to see one

large paw on the ground not far from me.

"You should be more worried about yourself, Princess," chided 'The Mad Scientist'. "I am now going to take you to King Kaarn."

"Why would Kaarn want to bother with her?" Yaani asked. "Why don't we just kill her and the others?"

"Because he can use them," Raavalla replied dismissively. "Our soft-hearted Princess will do anything to save her friends - including ordering her troops to surrender. You, Yaani, must know her weaknesses after your encounter with her on Earth."

Suddenly it came to me. "You're the red-headed girl who was going to throw Waggles into the water."

"Yes," Raavalla confirmed. "That was just a ruse to trick you. We knew that you'd want to rescue the mutt and take him home. We'd already bugged him."

"You wicked people!" I cried out. "But surely you don't want to be ruled by Kaarn? My Uncle Jamas told me how an operation turned him into a monster."

"That's not true," she snapped. "Kaarn experienced severe changes after undergoing life-saving surgery, similar to the more advanced operation I performed on your dog. At the time our scientists had just started experimenting by introducing genes into androids and they reversed the process to save Kaarn. There were some unfortunate side effects, but it has made him the strongest and most intelligent ruler in the world."

"But how can you support him, Raavalla, when he's

killed so many of your people?"

"There, you said *your* people," she retorted. "You don't feel like one of us, do you? I will never help you, Earth girl. Thaasia doesn't need a foreign Princess. I'm stronger than you will ever be and it's time you met the true ruler of Thaasia. I've told him we have you as our prisoner and we are now taking you to see him. Let's untie her and put her on the spare hoverboard."

Mikkel pulled me roughly to my feet and started to untie me. Before he had finished Raavalla came up and tore the communication bracelet from my arm, ripping my flesh in the process. "You won't need this," she said, ignoring my pain, and tossing the bracelet on the ground.

I was lifted by Mikkel on to one of the levitating boards. "Shall I remove the blindfold?" he asked.

"NO," bellowed Raavalla. "Just switch her hoverboard to 'auto' and then secure her with a light beam. The transporter would be quicker but we don't want to risk losing any more body parts, do we Mikkel?"

I promptly fell off my board! As I sprawled on the ground I guessed my bracelet was nearby and tried to feel for it, but 'The Mad Scientist' kicked it away.

"Nice try," she mocked. "Now no more tricks or I will send Yanni back to kill one of your friends. We are due to meet King Kaarn in precisely twelve minutes where the cave leads to the steps from the castle so we can't waste any more time."

Mikkel lifted me back on to the hoverboard and it

seemed a tight belt had been placed around my waist. "Don't worry," said Raavalla, "We are now using a light beam to control you."

Even though Mikkel was guiding me from behind with this circular beam, I found it hard to keep my balance as we set off along the tunnel and twice reached out to grasp Yanni in front of me.

Fortunately, the cave's rocky surface and continual curves prevented us going fast, but I was worried that we were steadily increasing the distance from where we had left Antony and the others.

I had to do something! I feigned to brush some hair from my forehead and, in doing so, tried to pull the blindfold down, but it only moved slightly. I began to gather my thoughts and willed the mist to return to my eyes. Instead of a deep purple, a lighter mist gathered, and I found I could see through the frayed binding.

"Almost there!" Raavalla told us.

I had to make my move soon. A few yards ahead was a narrow passage on the right and I dived into it, stretching the beam around my waist to breaking point. I pulled off the mask, used my purple mist to break the beam and turned to face my three enemies as they came after me.

Conjuring up the most powerful mist I had ever produced, I lifted all three of them off the ground, spinning them around in the air.

Yanni pulled out her gun and fired at me but the rays bounced back as they encountered my mist and hit her full in the chest. I moved back as Raavalla tried to kick me in the face and then bounced her along the ceiling. I blinked, causing the purple mist to fade, letting her fall, head first, to the floor. Mikkel grabbed hold of me but I glared at him so fiercely that the mist drove him against a shaft of rock sticking out from the wall. It went straight through his back.

I looked at their bodies in disbelief. I could see that Yanni and Mikkel were dead, their eyes staring lifelessly towards me. Raavalla was moaning and began to crawl back towards the cave, but, upon reaching it, she collapsed.

Before I could gather my thoughts, there was the sound of voices coming from behind me and footsteps approaching.

CHAPTER 44

I moved further down the passage but it was short and came to an abrupt end. So I pressed myself against the winding wall, out of sight from the main cave.

Within seconds Raavalla had been discovered.

"They'll pay for this," a voice boomed. "Find them and kill them all, every last one! I want no survivors."

"Yes, Sire," someone replied as a group of men stood around the fallen body a few feet away from me. "But shouldn't we take the Princess alive? We can use her to force the enemy to surrender."

"Don't argue with me, Orfuus. Once the Princess is dead the rebels will give up the battle."

"But if we take her prisoner..."

I heard a blast, followed by the acrid smell of burning, and the sound of a body crashing to the ground. Orfuus lay on the floor next to Raavalla, blood streaming from his head. I heard him splutter and breathe his last breath.

I've never been so frightened in my entire life. My heart thudded in my chest, making it difficult to breathe. I wanted to take large gasps of air but had to remain quiet.

"Does anyone else want to question me?" boomed the voice again.

No one spoke.

The deep evil voice sent chills through me. I was sure I was only a few seconds from being discovered and forced to meet my evil Uncle Kaarn, the man who had murdered my parents and now killed one of his own men.

"Round up our enemies and chop off their heads. We'll put them on stakes at the top of the castle for everyone to see. None of them must survive. I need you to bring me the girl NOW, Riickter. You've had years to find my brother's brat, *years*.

"Please be patient Your Majesty. Raavalla is still alive - she can tell us where the Princess is."

I could see him bend over the fallen scientist and talk to her. She murmured "I was bringing the Princess to you, Sire. She is... she's behind you." With that Raavalla collapsed in a heap.

"She's dead," announced Riickter.

"Behind me?" queried Kaarn. "The Princess must have fled back towards the cave entrance." Having clearly misunderstood Raavalla's last words and not aware I was only a few feet away. he promptly sent five of his troops running back down the cave to look for me.

Kaarn continued to rage. "I blame you for this Riickter. You had plenty of time to kill her and her minders."

"With respect, Sire, we needed to locate her rebel army first. We were able to follow the boy Antony back to Earth, and Yanni planted the dog that enabled us to track the spaceship bringing them to Thaasia. That's how we found out about her plans."

"Her plans*?* She had none - it was all *planned* out for her, you fool. All you had to do was *kill* her before she could come back to Thaasia. Why wait until she returned here?"

"But Sire, the more information we gathered the better our chances were of catching all her followers, not just the Princess. Finding where their ships were based was vital. And thanks to Raavalla's warning we are currently thwarting their attack and preventing them reaching the castle. Our ships have already shot down many of theirs."

From my hiding place I saw Kaarn turn, allowing me a better view of his mean features. He was huge, at least eight foot tall. His face was bloodless, his lips were cruel and curled into a snarl, but the most evil feature he possessed were his eyes. These large, black orbs looked like they belonged to a dead man. I was terrified.

Kaarn stepped menacingly towards Riickter and I could hear him grinding his teeth.

"I want the girl! You've got one more chance, Riickter, one last chance. If you fail me again you will suffer the same fate as Orfuus."

"I won't let you down, Sire."

"You had better not - time is running out for you."

"Perhaps I only need a single minute, Sire," replied his second in command as a flash of inspiration seemed to strike him. "Just one minute." He strode purposefully towards the passageway, no doubt realising what Raavalla had meant when she said "behind you".

He saw me and turned triumphantly to announce: "I have found her, Sire. You can come out now, Princess."

I gingerly emerged to find myself looking first at the smiling Riickter and then into the monstrous black eyes of the dreaded Kaarn.

"Don't be shy, Annaaqualalia. Come and say 'hello' to your uncle."

*****

As I moved hesitantly towards Kaarn my fear was suddenly overcome by anger. Purple lights flew from my eyes and surrounded him, but the mist I created had no effect.

He laughed cruelly. "So Annaaqualalia, you have little magic tricks like your mother, but they didn't save her, did they? And it will take more than that to hurt me. *Your* flesh is weak whereas I have hardly any human flesh left on my body so I can resist you. Would you like to see?

One of Kaarn's huge hands swept over his face and, with a sudden click, he removed it like a mask. Underneath were grotesque metal features. There were no eyebrows, two round holes where his nostrils had been, and thin, shiny metallic lips.

But the manic eyes remained. They were now focused fully on me and suddenly lit up. "I'll show you what real power is," he stormed. His glowing eyes produced a red laser light, which flashed inches from my head and smashed into the cave wall behind me.

I was preparing to meet my end when there was an enormous commotion as Jamas, Lee, Graham and Antony suddenly emerged to attack Riickter and the four other men still guarding Kaarn.

The King was only briefly distracted before he glared at me again. "Good-bye Princess," he said coldly, and released another laser light from his piercing eyes. But Lee, blood streaming down his left cheek from a wound he must have received earlier, leapt between us, taking the full force of the ray in his shoulder.

Kaarn cursed his fallen enemy, a spray of spit spewing out of his metal lips. He now focused his deadly eyes on Lee, who was lying on the ground in agony.

A terrible scream suddenly erupted behind Kaarn. It came from Antony. He launched himself on top of the eight foot giant who had just wounded his father. Taken by surprise, Kaarn toppled over, smashing his metal face against a piece of gagged rock, as Antony clung onto his neck, trying to throttle him. But the powerful King twisted his body violently and shrugged his assailant off like he was a rag doll.

A strong pair of arms encircled me from behind, and pulled me back out of harm's way.

They belonged to Uncle Jamas.

"Come with me, Annique. Thank God we regained consciousness in time to overcome Kaarn's men and race to your rescue."

"No, no - I can't leave Antony," I shouted.

Jamas continued to drag me away as I struggled, but he was grabbed by one of Kaarn's men and had to fight him off. This gave me the chance to run to the aid of my beloved friend.

Kaarn, despite having damaged his left eye in his fall, was standing over Antony, kicking him repeatedly, and preparing to finish him off by firing his laser into his head. I lashed out at the terrible tyrant, who turned to face me.

"Well, Annaaqualalia, you certainly have plenty of spirit. But now you must die. You are the last obstacle to be disposed of in order to ensure everything is mine." His deranged laugh echoed around the cave.

Antony frantically grabbed hold of Kaarn's leg, only to receive another kick in the head.

"Which one of you two shall I kill first?" the tyrant asked with relish, looking at Antony and then me. "Ladies first," he added, aiming the laser at my heart.

But he was knocked off his feet by a vicious thump in the back, and a voice yelling "No, you're the one who is going to die, Kaarn." It was Uncle Jamas. Holding a laser gun in both hands, he pulled the trigger and fired one loud blast. Kaarn dropped his weapon and rolled on to the floor, having sustained painful injuries to both his body and his pride.

"I have waited so long for this moment..." gloated Jamas. "...waited to avenge the deaths of my sister and her husband. Their daughter Annique will be queen in their place and peace will return to this planet once I've killed you."

"Jamas!" Kaarn blurted out. Then his shock gave way to sarcasm. "After all these years, we meet again. I thought you were dead, like your sister and Daald - but it seems you have been a gutless coward, hiding away on your own planet."

"That's where you are wrong. I've been here, helping the rebel army to rise up against you.

Now your awful reign is at an end. You are not flesh and blood like us, you're a metal shell taking instructions from an evil brain. This world will be a better place without you."

Jamas aimed at the tyrant's head and began to squeeze the trigger again. A blast echoed around the cave and blood came gushing out. But the blood was not the king's.

From behind us Riickter stood smiling at Kaarn, his laser still pointing at the falling Jamas.

"I said I would not let you down, Sire."

The evil black eyes of Kaarn slowly focused on me as he retrieved his own laser and pointed it at my chest.

"You will never be queen of this land."

I stared straight ahead, not wanting him to see my fear. I managed to release my purple mist but knew it would not be enough to save me. I wanted to thank all my friends before I died, though it was obviously too late for that.

The cruel king snarled again but before he could fire his laser a growl, as powerful as that of an angry lion, made us all turn.

An enormous creature launched itself ten foot into the air, knocking Kaarn onto his back.

Its large fangs tore deep into the metal face, gouging out the already damaged eye, before finally clamping around the King's large neck.

Kaarn screamed, trying to push the huge animal away, but Captain Waggles was no longer just a dog, he was a fighting machine, willing to give his life to protect me.

Black gunge spurted from Kaarn's head and neck. Letting out a series of horrifying screams from his now disfigured metallic mouth, he clawed frantically at his attacker. But the enraged Captain Waggles struck repeatedly with his huge teeth, ripping the fallen ruler into shreds.

Finally the defeated Kaarn lay in a heap of twisted metal on the floor. His tongue rolled back into what was left of his mouth and the remaining evil black eye seemed to be staring wildly up at the ceiling. He was dead.

There was an eerie silence as we all looked on, shocked, trying to take in what had just happened. It was broken by the panting of Captain Waggles and groans from the injured.

Graham had already disarmed Riickter, and Kaarn's other four guards had been over- powered.

I turned to see Antony trying to stem the blood from his father's wounds with his own shirt.

Next to him was my Uncle Jamas, his eyes closed. I

went over to him and cradled his head in my arms but he did not move.

Captain Waggles, now panting less frantically after his exhausting battle, came and sat with us and rested his enormous head between his paws.

"Thank you Waggles," I muttered, sobbing, "You saved my life, but you couldn't save Jamas."

"Don't cry," came a weak voice. It was my uncle's - he was still alive.

"Everything will be all right now, Annique," he whispered, opening his eyes. "That monster Kaarn is dead and you are safe. Have a good life and be happy. You will be a fine Queen for Thaasia." He reached out and took my hand. "Your Mother and Father would have been so proud of you," he coughed and blood appeared on his lips.

"There's a secret panel in your parents' chambers you should see. It is behind a painting of a unicorn, with red eyes, like rubies. Press them both at the same time and the panel will open."

"Shh," I said, kissing his brow tenderly and holding his hand. "You must rest. You'll get well soon, I know you will."

He sighed. "I wish that could be so Annique, but this is the end for me. Please help Kirsty take care of Saam. We have left him with her and Stella."

"We'll look after him, Uncle Jamas," I promised, tears running down my cheeks.

Jamas' head slowly fell back and he died in my arms.

CHAPTER 45

The next day bells started to ring everywhere as word spread that Kaarn was dead. People flooded onto the streets in their thousands to celebrate as they were no longer afraid. The hated orange and dark green flags on top of the castle were replaced with those of red and gold.

My main concern was to make sure that Stella was alright after she had been reactivated and given a new arm. Fortunately all had gone well with her 'surgery'.

I was then escorted to the royal apartments in a part of the palace that my parents had occupied before their deaths. Kaarn had sealed them off so they were covered in dust and smelled musty.

Sadness drifted over me as I entered their rooms, with Captain Waggles by my side. Clothes still hung in the cupboards, and on one wall was a picture of a white unicorn with a golden horn. I went over to it and, as Jamas had instructed, pressed the ruby red eyes at the same time. A panel on the wall sprung open, revealing a large cupboard with many boxes inside.

I took one of the smaller boxes over to my mother's dressing table and peered inside it to find two albums containing photographs. Near the front was one of a young lady with very straight black hair and purple eyes. She'd been giggling at something or someone behind the camera. I would never know what or who. On the same page in someone's handwriting was my mother's name Lalia, and a lock of black hair in a tiny velvet pouch.

The second album contained many photos from the two years I spent with my parents. We always seemed to be laughing. It was bitter sweet for me to look at them now. The last photo was of a group of people and among them, standing at the back, was Stella. She looked exactly the same then as she did today. It then occurred to me that Stella would probably outlive me just as she had my Mother and Father. She had been a wonderful guardian to all three of us, along with Graham, and I loved her so much.

I kissed my parents' faces so many times before putting the lid back on and going to choose another box. It contained papers and even older photos of three little boys. I turned them over, one by one, and read the names on the back: Daald, Thaa and Kaarn.

Then I picked up a leather-bound dairy, bearing Daald's name, and started to read it. Daald told in detail how tragedy had struck the royal family, beginning with his mother dying while giving birth to his brother Kaarn.

One passage read: "Life is so cruel. The terrible boating accident, which caused my brother Thaa to drown and my other brother Kaarn to become seriously ill, has left myself and my father devastated. My father is heart-broken and I fear he will not recover."

Another of Daald's diaries told how his father King Paactus died and he struggled to cope with the enormous task of succeeding him as our ruler soon after his 16th birthday. But Daald's life was turned around by meeting his beloved Lalia.

There were also many references to his brother Kaarn - how surgery had enabled him to make an amazing recovery but seemed to change him completely. Daald had written: "The crannos that saved Kaarn have taken away the loving brother I used to know."

Captain Waggles came up and rubbed against my leg. I gently put my hand on his head, tickling him under his ear. The old scar where they had planted the bugging device was still evident, but it did not seem to trouble him. The only problem was he was so large he kept bumping into things - and he knocked the diaries on to the thickly-carpeted floor.

While I was picking them up, a knock on the door startled me. But, the knowledge that Kaarn's followers had either been killed or surrendered, made me realise that I had nothing to fear. "Come in," I called.

Stella entered the room, bowing her head as she walked towards me.

"How are you feeling?" I asked. "Are you happy with your new arm?"

"Yes, it's much better than the previous one. I will have to go for some more adjustments after being reactivated, but I will be fine. After having two new arms

189

fitted - the latest models – I am fitter than I've every been. Now I must attend to my duties. This room is filthy - I'll have it cleaned and fresh linen put on your bed."

"Oh Stella, soon you'll be wearing your old pink apron again. I'm so glad you are still a mother to me. Please don't ever leave."

She smiled. "It would be an honour to serve you for the rest of your life if that is your wish Annique."

There was another knock at the door. Stella went to see who it was, and a familiar voice said: "Hi Stella, can I come in?"

It was Antony. As he approached me he bowed his head. He looked quite smart for a change.

"How is your father?" I asked.

"His wound is still being treated but the doctors say he will recover. How about you?"

"Strangely enough, Kaarn failed to seriously hurt me. My wrist is still sore where Raavalla tore the skin when ripping off my bracelet, but that's just a scratch compared to your father's injury."

"Yes, he'll be in hospital for some time and will miss your coronation. There is a lot to do before you are crowned. Mum says hundreds of people will be attending it. She has offered to help you in any way she can - at the moment she is looking after little Saam. She says she would be willing to act as his guardian if you are agreeable."

"That would be a great idea, wouldn't it Stella?"

"Yes," Stella replied. "I am sure Kirsty would make a perfect guardian for him. And that will leave Graham and I free to plan your coronation with Commander Geddaall. The date for that has been set for four weeks' time on April 24th."

I gulped. Thinking about the enormity of it both excited and scared me. Would I be able to cope with such a huge occasion - and a new life as a queen?

CHAPTER 46

After dinner, Antony and I sat on my balcony, looking up into the early evening sky and watching a large purple moon starting to emerge.

Little lights started to appear on the castle walls. "This planet gets its energy from the purple moon," he told me. "It's so beautiful," I said. "I'm finding it hard to take everything in after our dreadful confrontation with Kaarn. You and your father and Uncle Jamas saved my life. Antony, you were so brave to fight him."

Captain Waggles barked.

"Sorry, Waggles. You, too, of course. I swear you understand every word I say."

He pricked up his ears, clearly not fully placated. "OK, OK," I said. "You were a hero, too. If it wasn't for you that monster would have killed me."

Antony grinned. "You were very brave as well, Annique," he said. "Now you have got to show a different type of bravery to become Queen of Thaasia."

"I hope I can. It's going to be a huge task."

"But you won't be facing it alone, Annique. Graham and Stella will be a great help - and my parents and I will also be there to give our full support. We all love you."

"As long as I have you, Antony, I will be able to cope," I said, kissing him tenderly on the cheek.

CHAPTER 47

All these years later Antony still calls me Annique in our private moments together.

Everyone else refers to me as Queen Annaaqualalia, but to my husband I am 'Annique'.

We married two years ago and now have delightful twins, Paaline and Maarkus.

When we are not performing a royal duty we sit together in my parents' old apartments, now newly decorated but homely and comfortable. Saam, whose family did not survive the war with Kaarn, lives with us, and the twins love him. He says he wants to be an explorer when he grows up and travel all around Thaasia.

Captain Waggles has his own couch where most of the time he dozes, snoring loudly, nose twitching, but Saam takes him for walks both before and after school. I think Stella has also become quite fond of Waggles, though she denies it when I ask her, But little tit-bits of food keep appearing on his couch after she has been in the room, and he only gets fed the very best cuts of meat.

After the children have gone to bed, Antony and I go to our favourite balcony. Hand in hand, we stand looking up at the purple moon together and talk about the amazing changes in our lives. We still have fond memories of Earth and our friends there. We wish we could have brought our horses Crispin and Bella with us - riding Zaaks on Thaasia is not the same and they bite! Sometimes we even talk about our old school and I wonder what happened to Fizz and her gang.

Facing up to bullies like them and Kaarn has made me so much stronger. I am now able to cope with ruling a whole planet!

Stella runs the palace as efficiently as she used to look after our home in England. We don't see much of Graham because he has taken over the Laboratory where he spends virtually every day.

Kirsty and Lee have created a care home for children whose parents were killed in the battles with Kaarn's army. These orphans include those who survived after being snatched from their original families under the King's brutal ruling that did not allow mothers to have a third child.

My first action upon becoming queen was to change the law regarding the number of children each family could have. My new ruling meant families no longer had to give up their third child to the state and no child would be killed. Never again would children be separated from their parents and suffer such an awful fate.

My heart still breaks when I think of the children who had been terminated and used as spare parts.

We now have a special day when we celebrate all

births in the year. Each village has their own naming ceremony. Flags are flown, games are played - it's wonderful. We joined in when our own children Paaline and Maarkus were born and flags covered the castle.

Life is so hectic for Antony and I, but performing our royal duties is a pleasure.

Each night when I gaze at the purple moon I silently repeat to myself the question I had asked when I first arrived on Thaasia.

'Do I belong here?'

The answer is a resounding 'Yes'. With Antony, our children, Saam, Captain Waggles, my friends and loyal subjects giving me so much happiness, there is nowhere I would rather be.

TWINS CHAPTER 1

'Androids have no imagination', thought Maarkus.

Stella, his Mum's guardian android, had put a mural of a green, fire-breathing dragon on one of his bedroom walls as a surprise for his ninth birthday. And she'd painted the rest of the walls pale blue. He was gutted!

He'd have chosen orange instead of this boring shade of blue! And why did Stella think he'd want a dragon on his wall? There were enough pictures of them on the flags waving all over Thaasia - and they no longer existed.

"They're so old hat," Maarkus muttered as he ran along the hall to his twin sister Paaline's room to see her birthday treat.

After barging through her bedroom door he stood staring at the bright yellow walls. Her surprise mural was a castle with a rainbow glistening above it and market stalls in the grounds below. Just like the ones in the square outside their castle.

It was amazing! So once again Paaline had been treated better than him. As the first born, his sister would succeed their mother, Queen Annaqualalia, to the throne.

She, unlike him, had also inherited the Queen's gift of performing levitation by conjuring up purple mists to make objects - or people - rise in the air.

His aggravating sister added to Maarkus' frustrations by cheating when they played tennis and football, making the ball rise in the air above his head.

How he longed to be able to do levitation, too. He'd have such fun with the purple mist or falarge as his parents called it. But Dad had explained that the power to create the magical purple mist was only given to the female line of the family. So it had been passed on from his great-grandmother to his grandmother, mother and sister. This was because his great-grandmother had come from another planet called Riola, where women also had the power to hypnotise.

Life was so unfair - and goodness knows how much worse it would be when Paaline learned to perform hypnotism. She was sure to practice on him first.

TWINS CHAPTER 2

"What are you doing in my room Maarkus?" Pauline had suddenly appeared behind him.

"Just looking at your mural," he said. "It's amazing. It's got a castle, market stalls and people. Have you seen mine? It's only got a dragon. I'd love to run a stall myself and sell all sorts of unusual stuff."

"Don't be so silly Maarkus, you can't do that. You're a prince. You'd never be allowed to sell 'stuff' as you call it on a stall."

"I don't see why not. I could make jelly monster sweets looking just like the real ones who live in the caves and..."

Before he could continue, Captain Waggles bounded into the room and almost knocked him over. "Get down, boy!" Maarkus shouted as the huge dog gave him a slobbery lick on his face.

"Oh, I've just remembered," said Paaline. "Mum told me that she and Dad had to go to a special ceremony today. They are out planting trees in memory of those who died in the war against King Kaarn. I think they're planting a special one for Uncle Jamas."

"OK. When they come back I'll ask them if Gerzils

can be painted on my wall instead of dragons."

"Gerzils?"

"Jelly monsters. You must remember the story about the jelly monsters in the caves below the castle."

"Oh yes, I remember, but what's wrong with dragons?"

"They're old, ancient and no longer exist. I'd rather have a picture of huge jelly monsters with big mouths and yellow eyes."

"Perhaps they no longer exist, either," his sister scoffed.

"Yes they do. They're in the caves under this castle. Saam told me all about them before he went off to Space Academy. He said one of them exploded on Mum and Dad as they tried to get into the castle at the beginning of the great battle against Kaarn."

"That doesn't mean they're still there."

"Well, why don't we go down to the caves and have a look," he challenged.

"No thank you - those caves must be freezing cold."

"Ok, I'll take Captain Waggles."

TWINS CHAPTER 3

Maarkus sometimes thought that Captain Waggles understood him better than his own parents. The faithful dog trotted along behind him as the young prince strode down to the bottom of the castle and found the entrance to the caves.

He had remembered to bring a torch with him, but it was so dark that progress was slow and Maarkus had to slide his hands along the cold, dank walls. Paaline was right, it was also freezing.

As conditions became worse, Captain Waggles began to growl and came to a halt. But Maarkus refused to stop. "Come on, old boy - don't be scared. Saam told me that you got covered in slime by a jelly monster, but there's no sign of them. I'm sure we would smell them if they were near. Saam said they stunk."

The large dog immediately started sniffing - long, noisy sniffs - but didn't move.

"Well, if you can't smell them, let's go on."

The dog walked along warily, placing his paws gingerly on the rough ground, strewn by rocks and pebbles. When he trod in a large puddle he sprung back in alarm, landing with all four paws splayed in different directions.

"Come on, you silly dog. It's a puddle - not a cold jelly monster."

Captain Waggles finally followed Maarkus, sniffing and looking left and right. Slowly and quietly they crept further into the cave. The torch sent a beam of light cascading along the tunnel, but failed to alert Maarkus to a large droplet of water which fell on his face, temporarily blinding him.

He stumbled and fell heavily against the side of a rocky wall which suddenly gave way, causing him to tumble into a hidden part of the cave. Captain Waggles leapt forward and took a chunk of the prince's coat in his mouth to prevent him going any further into the darkness.

When Maarkus finally wiped the water from his eyes he levered himself to stand upright.

"Come on, Captain Waggles. I can see a tunnel ahead. You can stop tugging at my coat now. I'm going to see if this leads anywhere."

The dog followed, whining softly through gritted teeth.

Maarkus slowly and carefully walked along the dark tunnel, keeping his left hand pressed against the wall. The passage ahead began to glow with a strange green light which grew more luminescent as they continued.

The light seemed to be coming from a large oval object in the side of the wall ahead. It was an egg. Maarkus cautiously put out his right hand, feeling slight waves softly bouncing off his fingers. Finally he touched the hard shell.

The green glow intensified, warming his hand.

'I wonder what's in the egg', he thought. 'Could it be a bird or a lizard? It's so big - perhaps there are dragons, after all'.

TWINS CHAPTER 4

Suddenly there was a loud crack above Maarkus' head and boulders came crashing down around him. Three of them fell on top of him, pinning his left leg and foot to the ground.

Captain Waggles had escaped just in time by leaping backwards.

Ignoring his pain, Maarkus tried in vain to free himself, but without success. He finally gave up and shouted to the barking dog: "Go back to the castle and get help."

Captain Waggles turned tail and did as he was told.

After what seemed an eternity Waggles returned with Paaline.

Maarkus sighed. "It's good of you to come, Sis. But I had hoped Captain Waggles would bring a couple of hefty servants as well."

"You seem to forget, dear brother, that I have magic powers. Let me try to move the rocks."

Paaline focused her eyes on the solid mass on top of her brother and surrounded it with a pale purple mist, but the boulders did not move.

"This is hopeless," moaned Maarkus.

"Have faith," said Paaline, focusing again. This time a

deep rich purple mist appeared. The rocks, surrounded by the mist, began to rise and Maarkus was able to crawl out from under them before they crashed back to the ground, leaving a cloud of grey dust floating into the air.

Paaline hadn't noticed the egg, which was no longer glowing, and Maarkus decided not to mention it. Leaving the egg behind, they made their way back to the castle, with Maarkus hobbling along on his injured ankle.

TWINS CHAPTER 5

Maarkus spent the rest of the day on his bed, resting his leg and ankle.

Maybe he'd been wrong to be envious of his sister and her powers. They could be very useful and he had to admit he was grateful to her.

When his parents returned they came to his room and were shocked to learn he had hurt himself.

Maarkus reluctantly told them about his adventure in the caves, but did not mention the egg. He had every intention of sneeking back to investigate further when he recovered.

His parents, who sat on the edge of his large bed, had other ideas. "You were lucky not to suffer a more serious injury," said his mother. "It's a good job that Captain Waggles managed to get Paaline to come to your rescue," She patted the dog which was laying on the floor.

"Yes," added Antony. "Those caves can be dangerous. You are not to go into them again."

"Oh, Dad. Please don't say that," Maarkus pleaded.

"I mean it. If you had run into a Gerzil goodness knows what would have happened. Do you remember the old rhyme I told you?

"The Gerzil is watching, take care or he'll come,

He sees all the bad things you do, every one.

Don't try to hide from his big yellow eyes,

They will see right through any disguise"

They all laughed but his mother stressed: "You must never go into the caves on your own again, Maarkus. Do you hear me?"

"Yes Mum, okay."

Annique turned to look at the picture of the dragon on the wall behind her. "You haven't told me what you think of the mural."

Maarkus hesitated.

"I love mine," said Paaline, butting in. "But I don't think Maarkus likes his so much."

Her brother looked again at the painting and smiled. "I'm growing to like it and, who knows - dragons might come into fashion again."

About the Author

Heather Flood was encouraged to write by her husband Tony, a former journalist.

She began by reviewing theatrical productions for the Richmond and Twickenham Times series and still pens theatre reviews for the Brighton Argus.

Heather gave Tony the idea for his first novel, fantasy adventure SECRET POTION, and then decided to write children's books herself, mainly for her grandchildren.

She started with the MOUSEY MOUSEY series featuring a lovable lady mouse and followed that with GIANT STICKER MONSTER AND OTHER CHILDREN'S STORIES.

Heather, pictured here with Tony, has benefited from belonging to the Anderida Writers Group in Eastbourne, with whom she has won awards. She also loves singing and belonged to the Concentus choir for several years.

Heather enjoys new challenges. These have included helping her first husband build three houses, climbing The Great Wall of China and making her son's wedding cake.

You can find details about Heather and Tony's books on **www.fantasyadventurebooks.com | www.celebritiesconfessions.com**